AVENGING ANGEL

A woman and child were about to cross the road but, seeing Angelo, stopped. There was a look of fear on the woman's face which Angelo couldn't understand. Then the engine noise was upon him and he realized why they were scared. He looked round quickly. There was a car coming at him, way too fast. The woman and child both screamed.

The car was almost upon him. Angelo could see the panicked face of the driver. He tried to throw himself out of the way, into the row of stationary cars in the other lane. But he didn't have time. For a moment, the whole world went black. When his vision returned, the car had gone. Angelo was on the road, with his bike on top of him, in agonizing pain . . .

POINT CRIME

AVENGING ANGEL

David Belbin

Cover illustration by David Wyatt

■SCHOLASTIC

For John Harvey

Scholastic Children's Books,
Scholastic Publications Ltd,
7-9 Pratt Street, London NW1 0AE, UK

Scholastic Inc.,
555 Broadway, New York, NY 10012-3999, USA

Scholastic Canada Ltd,
123 Newkirk Road, Richmond Hill,
Ontario, Canada L4C 3G5

Ashton Scholastic Pty Ltd,
PO Box 579, Gosford, New South Wales,
Australia

Ashton Scholastic Ltd,
Private Bag 92801, Penrose, Auckland,
New Zealand

First published by Scholastic Publications Ltd, 1994

Text copyright © David Belbin, 1994

ISBN 0 590 55310 0

Typeset by TW Typesetting, Midsomer Norton, Avon
Printed by Cox & Wyman Ltd, Reading, Berks.

10 9 8 7 6 5 4 3 2

1

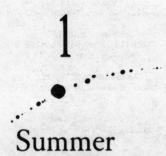

Summer

Prologue

Angelo Coppola left the paper shop, threw his fluorescent yellow bag around his shoulders, and mounted his bike.

"Hey, Angel!"

Angelo cringed, then nodded at Carol Ward, one of the other paper deliverers. Carol was always teasing him. Angelo hated his Christian name. He'd heard every different nickname that you could possibly make out of it: Angel Features, Angel-face, etcetera, etcetera. Older people were always embarrassing him by commenting that the name fitted his clean-cut looks. He would never forgive his mum and dad for calling him Angelo. Didn't they realize what they were doing?

It would have been much more sensible if they'd

called his sister Clare "Angela". Clare, five years older than him, could look angelic on occasion. She was tall, with deep blue eyes and long, flowing black hair. Why did they have to name her after Mum's mother? Oh no: the family name had to go to the boy. Dad claimed it was an Italian family tradition.

Traffic was building up on Alfreton Road. Angelo was late starting his paper round because he'd been round at Paul's, playing Subbuteo. It was halfway through the long summer holiday. He and Paul were playing an entire FA Cup series and this afternoon was the first Quarter Final. The game went into extra time before Angelo's Sheffield United beat Paul's Chelsea, five–four.

Sometimes the road was too busy for Angelo to cross it on a bike. It was quicker to cross at the pedestrian lights instead. Today, however, the two lanes behind Angelo were clear. He cycled over into a third, right-turning lane. On the other side of the road, both lanes of traffic going into town were backed up. He would be able to weave between the cars onto Bobbers Mill Road, where his round began.

The cars behind Angelo on his right began to move, but the two nearest the road entrance stayed put, leaving a gap for the bike to get through. Angelo raised his hand in thanks and cycled through the gap. As he did so, one of the cars sounded its horn. Why?

A woman and child were about to cross the road but, seeing Angelo, stopped. There was a look of fear on the woman's face which Angelo couldn't understand. Then the engine noise was upon him and he realized why they were scared. He looked round quickly. There was a car coming at him, way too fast. The woman and child both screamed.

The car was almost upon him. Angelo could see the panicked face of the driver. He tried to throw himself out of the way, into the row of stationary cars in the other lane. But he didn't have time. For a moment, the whole world went black. When his vision returned, the car had gone. Angelo was on the road, with his bike on top of him, in agonizing pain.

1

Summer had lasted too long. That afternoon, the patrol car's calls had included: a bunch of joyriders who'd managed to boost a Jag; two sets of drunks who refused to leave city pubs; a streaker on Maid Marian Way and a knife fight bang in the middle of Slab Square, the heart of the shopping centre. Still, it was sweltering. As the evening began, more tempers would fray. When it got this hot, violent domestics sky-rocketed and the smallest traffic incident could turn into World War Three. Neil Foster was glad that today's shift was nearly over.

He looked at his watch. Ten to five.

"I could do with a break for something to eat soon," he told Jan, who was driving.

His partner made no comment, but turned left onto the Boulevard, where the home-time traffic was at its peak. They were nearly at the junction with Alfreton Road now: a major bottleneck with a left filter and an illegal right turn. They would be stuck here for up to five minutes. Jan began to drum her fingers on the steering wheel. Then a message from the traffic department came through on the radio.

"RTA Junction of Alfreton Road and Bobbers Mill Road. Possible fatality."

Jan radioed back.

"Unit 63 responding."

She switched on the siren, but there was nowhere for the cars in front to get out of their way. Neil unbuckled his seat belt.

"I'll run over there. It'll be quicker."

Jan nodded. Neil got out of the car and ran towards the scene of the RTA. He would be there in two minutes, provided he could get across the busy four lanes of traffic.

Meanwhile, Jan sat behind the wheel, frustrated. The accident couldn't have happened at a worse place, at a worse time. The cars in front tried to get out of her way, some moving into the centre of the road, some pulling onto the kerb. She edged the Panda forward in the narrow gap that they had created.

Neil would be at the accident by now. She hoped

that he would do his job properly. He could be impulsive. Sometimes that was good, like the initiative he'd just shown in running over to the accident. But other times he was careless. He had only been on the job eight months, to her eight years. She was his "mentor" and, since her promotion two months before, his sergeant, too.

She was at the lights now. Cars stopped to let her through. Jan accelerated a hundred metres down the road. The cars on the other side of the road were all stationary, bumper to bumper, except for a small gap where a knot of people stood, gaping at something.

That was where the accident was.

As Jan got out of the car, people moved back off the road. That left Neil Foster and the victim, a boy dressed in T-shirt and jeans, with trainers. Next to him lay a mangled bicycle. The boy looked about thirteen – fourteen at the most. Round his shoulders was a bright yellow newspaper bag with *Evening Post* written across it. Neil was giving him the kiss of life.

Jan turned her attention to the onlookers, who were standing sheepishly by the side of the road.

"Did the car stop?" she asked.

They all began to speak at once. No, the car had not stopped. A hit and run. That was all Jan wanted to know for now. If the car was to be found, it would have to be quickly. Some of the people standing around were already beginning to walk off.

"I don't want anybody to leave!" she shouted at them. "We're going to need you as witnesses. That includes you, sir."

A middle-aged man in a cheap off-the-peg suit stopped by the chip shop, looking guilty.

"Did anybody get a good look at the car?" Jan asked. "I need the colour, the make, the number plate . . ."

There was a babble of replies. It was something you learned to do in this job – listen to a dozen people talking at once and pick out the one or two who actually knew what they were talking about. Unfortunately, the best witnesses were probably sat behind the wheels of their cars, at the front of the noisily expanding traffic jam. But Jan didn't have time to go round each one of them.

"It was green . . ."

"No, yellow . . ."

"A Ford."

"What kind of Ford?" Jan asked.

"A Sierra . . ."

"No, an Escort."

It was no good. There wasn't enough consensus among the witnesses for Jan to radio a description to headquarters. In the distance, she heard an ambulance siren. She turned to Neil. He was still leaning over the boy.

"How is he?"

Neil replied breathlessly.

"I think his chest's been crushed. There are head injuries, too."

Jan could see that. There wasn't a lot of blood, but that didn't mean it wasn't bad.

"Can you find any identification?"

Gently, Neil pulled a small pocket book from the boy's trousers. As he handed it to Jan, he spoke again.

"Just before he passed out, he said something."

"What?"

"It sounded like 'blaze'. Any idea what it might mean?"

Jan shook her head. As the ambulance pulled up, Neil began to give the boy the kiss of life again. Jan opened the pocket book. There was a bus pass with a photograph: a grinning, fresh-faced boy with short, blond hair. His name was Angelo Coppola. From his date of birth, it appeared that he had turned fourteen the month before. He lived only a few streets away.

The ambulance men had the boy, Angelo, on a stretcher. Further down the road, Jan could see three more police cars trying to get across two lanes of traffic, and failing.

"You'd better go with him," she said to Neil, "in case he recovers consciousness, can tell you something about the accident."

Neil did as she asked. Jan went to the front of the ambulance.

"What are his chances?" she asked the driver, as he got back in his seat.

Without looking at her, the man shook his head. Then he switched on the siren.

Jan sighed as the ambulance sped off. She walked slowly across the part of the road where it had happened, looking for fresh tyre marks. All she could see were endless newspapers strewn across the road, one of them bearing a small patch of blood. For no reason she could put words to, Jan picked this paper up. She put it under her arm and folded it so that the blood didn't show. Then she stepped onto the pavement and joined the waiting witnesses.

Clare Coppola was helping her mother prepare the evening meal. She sliced garlic thinly and tossed it into the pan, watching the heat carefully to ensure that it didn't burn. Mum came in from the garden with some basil leaves from the plant outside. Clare went to work on a red pepper while Mum took the biggest, sharpest knife from the rack and chopped the steak into precise two-centimetre cubes.

Clare checked the cooker clock. Five. She switched on the radio for the news. It was tuned to Radio Trent, the local commercial station, which

Mum liked best. Clare preferred the news on Radio Four. It had more depth. But the only time she'd suggested this to Mum, it was as though she'd proposed going to an Anglican church rather than a Catholic one. Mum *liked* all the minor local stories. She found the trite adverts informative. She even seemed to enjoy the endless traffic reports. It drove Clare crazy.

Clare chopped shallots to go with the peppers and opened a can of tomatoes. Mum was a bit behind schedule today, and Clare had offered to help, though she wasn't expected to. Dad would be home from work at six. He liked his dinner by half past – or seven at the very latest. Clare's brother had just got a paper round, so he was no use. Anyway, Clare quite liked cooking. She didn't find it demeaning, as some of her friends claimed to.

Now the announcer was saying: "And word is coming in of major hold-ups on the north side of the city. There's been an accident near the junction of Alfreton Road and Radford Boulevard. Police are still interviewing witnesses, so no traffic is moving at all, causing tailbacks on all northern routes into the city. Police say that it will be some time before traffic starts moving again."

"Your father'll be late," Mum said.

"Less hurry for us," Clare replied.

"You go back to your books. I can finish here."

Clare didn't feel like reading, but there was

nothing left for her to do in the kitchen, so she washed her hands and went into the front room. Maybe she would put a record on, drown out the boring radio. Also, Angelo would be back soon. If he got in the front room before she did, he would take over the TV set for his computer games, and she would be driven upstairs until dinner.

Clare wished that the summer vacation was over. There was another month before she could return to Manchester. The other week, she had mentioned the possibility of going back early. After all, her shared flat was available from the middle of September. Dad nearly blew his top. What was wrong with living at home, he wanted to know. Was she getting too high and mighty for her old friends and family? Who did she think had paid her share of the deposit on the flat?

Mum defended Clare. She pointed out that when she was Clare's age, she'd already left home. She'd married Dad, despite her parents' objections that Nick Coppola was a no-good Italian labourer.

However, Mum warned Clare: "There's no more money for you. It's a lot cheaper, living at home." Which was true. Practically all of Clare's friends were stuck with their parents. There were no summer jobs to be had. The grant wasn't even enough to keep you going in term time.

At twenty past five the doorbell rang. Clare went to the door. She assumed that it would be Angelo.

He'd have forgotten his key again. Clare wished that she had a part-time job. It would be better than scrounging off her father all the time. And it took seven years to qualify as an architect. She must have been crazy to—

She saw the dark figures on the other side of the glazed glass. It wasn't Angelo.

"Mum!"

Clare opened the door as Mum came through from the kitchen, complaining about the interruption. There were two of them, both in uniform – a man and a woman. The woman looked over Clare's shoulder and spoke directly to Mum. Clare stared at their faces, reading everything into them.

"Mrs Coppola?"

Clare turned to look at Mum, who was nodding, her eyes red with fear.

"May we come in, please?"

Mum kept nodding and Clare stepped aside. She could feel her stomach tightening as the policewoman spoke again.

"I'm afraid we've got some bad news . . ."

2

Mum was collapsed in Clare's arms, sobbing. Clare kept blinking, unable to react fully, almost numb. The policewoman was saying:

"We'll drive you to the hospital. What about Angelo's father? Does he live with you?"

"He'll be on his way home," Clare told her. "But with the traffic—"

"I can wait here for him," the policeman offered.

The policewoman was helping Mum to stand up. Clare thought about Dad, coming home to find a stranger with tragic news.

"Dad's a builder," she said, as though this was important. "He's got a mobile phone. I think it's best that I ring him, tell him to go straight to the hospital."

"Yes," said the policewoman. "I think that's a good idea. Will you be. . . ?"

Clare nodded. The policewoman gently guided Mum away. Clare went to the phone in the kitchen. The stew was starting to burn. She turned it down, then thought again, and turned it off. She dialled Dad's carphone number automatically, without thinking how she was going to put the news. What difference would well-chosen words make? The effect would be the same.

The phone rang three times before Dad answered.

"Yes, hello?"

"Dad, it's Clare."

"Clare? What is it?"

"It's Angelo, Dad. He's had an accident."

There was a pause. Clare knew that she couldn't tell Dad everything the policewoman had said. He would be too upset to drive to the hospital.

"How bad?" Dad asked.

"It's serious, Dad. A car knocked him off his bike. We won't know how bad it is until we get to the hospital. He's at the Queen's. The police are going to take Mum and me. Can you meet us there?"

Dad's voice became gruff, the way it always did when he was covering up emotion.

"Yes, yes. Where's Maria? Can I talk to her?"

"I don't think Mum's up to talking, Dad."

The policewoman had come back into the kitchen.

"I think we need to go, Dad."

"I'll be as quick as I can. The traffic's hell tonight, though."

"I know. Drive safely. I'll see you there. I love you, Dad."

"I love you, too."

Clare put the phone down. Her body was shaking. Tears streamed down her face. The police-woman put an arm around her.

"Come on, love. Let's take you to your brother."

"They're still operating," the nurse told Neil Foster, "but there's really no chance of him re-covering consciousness. You might as well leave."

Neil got up as though to go. He'd been waiting around in case Angelo Coppola was able to give a description of the car that hit him. Still, he was reluctant to go. He had held the boy in his arms, had spoken to him before he passed out. He ought to talk to the family before he went home.

They arrived two minutes later – mother and daughter, arms around each other. The mother was small, fortyish, with short brown hair. The daughter was much taller. She had long, thick black hair and was stunningly attractive, even though she'd been crying. The two women began to ask the nurse a lot of questions, which she avoided answering. To Neil's surprise, neither of them sounded Italian.

"This is Police Constable Foster. He was the first to reach Angelo. He gave him resuscitation, which may have been what kept him alive."

"Thank you," the mother said. "Thank you for helping our son."

Neil wanted to say "it was nothing", but didn't, because he knew that it *was* nothing and he didn't know if they knew that yet.

"What happened?" the girl asked. "No one seems terribly sure."

"A hit and run," Neil said. "A car cutting across the main road didn't see your brother in time. That's what it looks like, anyway."

"Was he in a lot of pain?" the girl asked.

"I don't think so. He was still conscious when I got to him. He said something to me. I don't know what it meant."

"What did he say?"

"Just one word: 'blaze'."

He looked at the girl. Her face was blank.

"Does that mean anything to you?"

The girl shook her head.

"The make of the car that hit him, maybe?"

"That occurred to me. We'll check it out."

They were interrupted by the arrival of a large, dark-haired man in a sweat-soaked, open-necked shirt. He spoke with a slight Italian accent.

"Maria, Clare. How is he?"

"They won't let us see him until they've finished operating, Nick," Maria said. "They say it's very bad – his head and his chest."

Nick Coppola hung his head.

"*Dio.*"

Neil shuffled uncomfortably as the three of them hugged. It was time for him to go. Nick Coppola broke away from the two women and spoke to Neil.

"You'll find him, won't you? You'll find the *stronzo* who did this to my son?"

"We'll do our best, sir."

A middle-aged man in a white coat was walking down the corridor. Neil recognized the surgeon who had been operating on Angelo Coppola. It was over already. Neil had hoped not to be here when this happened.

"I'm very sorry," the surgeon was saying to the Coppolas. "We did all that we could do, but his injuries were too severe. We lost him five minutes ago."

The father broke down first, then the daughter. The mother remained calm.

"Can we see him?" she asked. "Can you take us to my son?"

"Yes, of course."

The surgeon led them down the corridor.

Neil phoned Jan at the station. He told her what had happened.

"Any leads?" he asked, when he'd finished.

"Not enough to go on. The only thing the witnesses agree about is that it's a light-coloured car of 'normal' shape – not a hatchback, in other words. We're still interviewing people. Hopefully, something will come up. Why don't you get a meal before you come in? You deserve a break."

"Thanks, Jan, but I'm not hungry right now."

Neil stepped outside into the sweltering evening, thinking about the dead boy. He remembered his promise to the Coppolas. It was true. The police would do the best they could. But he knew from his training – if they hadn't got the car within an hour of the incident, the chances of catching the driver were poor.

Neil told the taxi-driver where he was going.

"Might take a while," the cabbie told him. "Traffic's murder tonight."

"You're right," said Neil. "It is."

3

"It's like I told you yesterday . . ."

"It's too hot to concentrate in here. Can't you turn that fan on?"

"I'm sorry, sir, it's broken."

Several witnesses were being interviewed for a second time. They weren't happy about it. The Traffic Superintendent had been informed of Angelo's death and he had put Inspector Thompson in charge of the investigation. It was Thompson who had insisted on the re-interviews. Jan and Neil were still on the case, but their opinion didn't seem to count for much.

"What about the boy's last word, sir, 'blaze'? Shouldn't we be checking that out?"

Thompson, a career policeman with a greying

moustache and a growing bald patch, gave Neil a supercilious look.

"You asked the family and it meant nothing to them, right?"

"That's right," Neil replied. "But I thought that it might be the model of the car that hit him, or even a design on the side of it. You know the way that some people—"

Thompson interrupted him.

"Think about it, lad. You're about to be run over by a big car, speeding straight at you. What do you do?"

Neil didn't reply. The Inspector carried on, his voice dripping with sarcasm.

"You don't drop your bike and run to try to somehow get out of its way. No, you stay there in the middle of the road and see if you can recognize the model of the car about to hit you. Smart move, eh? Mind you, if Coppola was in such an observant frame of mind, you'd think he'd have memorized the number-plates too, wouldn't you?"

Neil swallowed and tried again.

"Surely it's possible that he recognized the car in some way and was trying to tell me about it."

Thompson shrugged his broad shoulders.

"Possible, yes. Likely, no. We'll get to it when we have time, Foster. Now, do you think that you could interview Mrs Ohagi again?"

Neil went back to the interview room. Mrs Ohagi was a Nigerian woman who had been coming out of the chip shop on the corner of the road where Angelo Coppola was knocked down. The officer who first interviewed her had described her as a "very clear" witness.

"I've no idea of the make," she told Neil, "but the car was green, I'm sure about that."

"What shade of green?"

"Quite light. A sort of lime green, I think."

Neil made a note. This was an advance on the previous day.

"New? Old?"

She shook her head.

"Not old and rusty, but I'm not sure how new . . . you see, I was looking more at the boy. He was right in the middle of the road. There was no way that he could get out of the way in time. I think I screamed."

"Any idea what speed the car was doing?"

"I don't know. Forty? Fifty? It would have to have been pretty fast, wouldn't it?"

Neil nodded, though this wasn't strictly true. Ninety per cent of people hit by a car doing forty miles an hour died.

"What about the driver? Did you see who was behind the wheel?"

"Only a glimpse."

Again, she hadn't said this yesterday. Or, if she

had, the interviewing officer hadn't written it down.

"What can you tell me about the driver?"

"Not much."

"A man or a woman?"

"A woman, I think."

"Black or white?"

"White."

"Age?"

"No idea."

"What was she wearing?"

Mrs Ohagi paused.

"I'm not sure. No, wait. I think she might have had something on her head. Something bright. A headband, perhaps."

Neil let the silence linger, the way he'd been taught to, in case Mrs Ohagi's subconscious came up with another gem. Finally, he asked:

"Anything else?"

"Sorry, no. Even what I've just told you is very hazy. It was such a shock."

"And you say this woman was alone in the car?"

"Yes. I'm sure about that."

Neil offered her his hand.

"Thank you. Thanks for coming in. You've been a great help."

Jan was in a small terraced house on Hazelwood Road, five minutes' walk from the place where

Angelo Coppola had been fatally injured. She was interviewing one of the two people who'd been crossing the road at the same time as Angelo Coppola. Tracey Lord was a thin girl, barely out of her teens. She sat on the sofa, chewing gum, while her three-year-old daughter Jade played on the floor.

"Just take me through it again slowly, Tracey."

Tracey sighed.

"I don't see the point. I'm not going to re-member anything else. I keep telling you. I was just bothered about getting Jade out of that maniac's way!"

"You'd already started to cross the road?"

"I was on the road, yeah. The lad who was killed, he came across on his bike – cocky as any-thing, they are, those kids on bikes – he came right through the cars on Alfreton Road. Well, I wasn't going to get out of his way, but then I saw the car behind him. You know, if he'd heard it, he might have got out of the way, mightn't he? But it's really noisy along there, with all that traffic . . ."

Jan let Tracey go on in the way she wanted. Let a witness tell it her way, and it was possible that she'd come up with something she didn't know she remembered.

"Did you get a good look at the car?" Jan prompted.

"It just came from nowhere, dead fast, straight at us, you know, like a bullet, dead fast."

"Straight at *you*?"

Tracey nodded.

"I was sure it was going to hit me and Jade, yeah. But then it sort of swerved and went into the boy instead."

"You were still on the road? You didn't have time to get back onto the pavement?"

"Jade and me just stood still, on the edge of the road . . . he came this close."

She held out her arms to indicate a distance of less than a metre. The thin material of her cheap cotton blouse flapped around her shoulders. Jan wished that she was wearing lighter clothing. It was so hot that she found it hard to concentrate. Her head felt like mashed potatoes. It would be easy to miss something. She consulted her notes.

"He . . . you said 'he' just now."

"Yeah."

"Only, yesterday you said that you didn't see who was in the car at all, couldn't even remember what colour the car was."

Tracey stared into space. Jan couldn't tell if she was concentrating or her mind was as blank as she looked. Finally, she answered.

"Got to be a man, hasn't it? When did you ever hear of a woman driving like that?"

*   *   *

The road looked the same as ever. Traffic flowed smoothly. There was no sign of what had happened to Angelo there. Why should there be? It was important, Clare had decided, to come here quickly, to cross the road, to go to the shops, not to build up some kind of taboo about the place where her brother was knocked down.

Anyway, she couldn't stand it at home any longer. All day there had been calls of condolence. It was good to know that so many people cared. It kept Mum and Dad occupied, too. But it was driving Clare round the twist. She didn't want to hear one more person tell them how pointless Angelo's death was, how tragic. She wanted to be able to do something about it.

Clare had spent the morning fielding phone calls. Close friends were put through to Mum or Dad, if they could come to the phone. Business colleagues and more casual acquaintances, Clare spoke to herself.

Hardest to deal with were the calls from Italy. Clare's Italian was rusty, but Mum or Dad couldn't always come straight to the phone. Dad had phoned her uncle that morning. He'd agreed to tell the relatives in Napoli. Just before Clare left the house, her grandmother rang, immediately bursting into floods of tears.

Since the *Evening Post* came out there had been more calls. Clare told Mum and Dad she was going to buy a copy, see what it said. Now, as she walked into the shop, a silence descended. Mr Malik came out from behind the counter.

"We are so, so sorry. If there is anything we can do, anything . . ."

Clare nodded blankly.

"He was a good boy, Angelo, the best. He had so much life to live."

Clare picked up a paper off the counter. Mrs Malik came out from the back of the shop. Clare reached into the pocket of her jeans and realized that she didn't have her purse with her. Before she could explain this, Mrs Malik shook her head.

"Take it, please. Do you need anything else?"

Clare shook her head. Mrs Malik took Clare's arm and squeezed it.

"We feel so bad about what happened. If we hadn't taken Angelo on . . ."

"You mustn't even *think* that sort of thing," Clare said. "Only one person is to blame for what happened – whoever was behind the wheel of that car."

"I'm sure they'll find him," said Mr Malik.

"They'd better," Clare told him, clenching her fist beneath the newspaper. "They'd better."

Anger made her feel stronger. Instead of walking back to the house, she walked down the road a little, to Churchfield Lane. This was where the car which ran over Angelo had come from. It was a rat run. By cutting across Alfreton Road to Bobbers

Mill Road you could get to Hyson Green without meeting any traffic hold-ups. A lot of drivers did it, though, and, sometimes, like now, there was a queue of cars waiting to drive across the busy main road.

There was a patch of land at the end of Churchfield Lane, the one which gave the road its name. Clare sat there sometimes, in the shade of St Peter's Church, and sketched. Sometimes she drew the trees around her, sometimes the buildings. Other times she would draw cityscapes. Over the years, she had a record, not just of her improved drawing skills, but also of how the city had changed.

When Clare first visited the churchyard, there had been a giant Players Cigarette factory behind her. Now it was a retail park. All that remained of the old factory was its clock, set on a plinth in the corner. Clare sat down on a bench and looked at the paper for the first time. Angelo's death did not appear on the front page. She had to scan page three twice before she found the story, just beneath the fold of the broadsheet.

"HIT AND RUN" DRIVER SOUGHT
Police are appealing for the driver of the car which killed Angelo Coppola, 14, yesterday to come forward. Paperboy Angelo died from massive head and chest injuries within an hour of being knocked from his bike.

"We will find whoever is responsible for this death," said Inspector Brian Thompson, who is in charge of the investigation, *"and it will be easier for them if they give themselves up now, rather than making us spend numerous police hours on the investigation."*

Angelo was run over at the junction of Alfreton Road and Bobbers Mill Road, at ten to five yesterday afternoon. The incident caused grid-lock conditions on the north side of the city, delaying many drivers for over an hour.

Inspector Thompson thanked motorists for their patience and co-operation. *"We would appreciate it if any witnesses whom we have not interviewed would contact the Radford Road Police Station,"* he said. Angelo is survived by his parents, Nicholas and Mary, and his older sister, Clare.

It annoyed Clare that the paper had printed her parents' names that way – no one ever called Dad anything but Nick, and his full name was Niccolo, not Nicholas. Mum's parents were the only ones who still called her Mary – to everyone else she was Maria, the name which Dad gave her when they first started courting.

Clare got up and left the churchyard, thinking about Angelo. She and her brother weren't that close. There was five years between them. Clare had been an "accident", forcing her parents to marry before they were ready. Angelo was a planned baby, born shortly after Mum and Dad moved to the house where they still lived. Clare loved her brother, but she envied him, too. He always seemed to have so much more freedom than her.

Clare had expected that she and Angelo would become closer as they got older. The age difference would stop mattering so much. Now that would never happen. She'd been so happy when he was born, so keen that the new baby would be a boy.

Now she would never be able to give him the benefit of her experience in passing exams, never give him advice about his first girlfriend, never swap notes about how each of them *really* felt about different members of the family. He wouldn't be there at her graduation ceremony or her marriage. He would never be an uncle to her children.

Clare knew that she ought to be sad, but instead she was angry. She was so preoccupied with her anger that she started to cross the quiet road without looking. A horn sounded. She turned round to see a fast-moving Ford Escort coming out of nowhere.

As Clare stepped back onto the pavement, two teenage heads poked out of the back window and jeered at her: the usual insulting, sexist obscenities. She gave them the finger. It was the wrong thing to do. You didn't provoke louts. But she was mad. She didn't care.

The car squealed to a halt and did a "U" turn in the middle of the road. A yellow Escort. Clare stood her ground. She made herself memorize the first part of the licence plate number, Y642 ... The car hurtled towards her. What could these lads do? she thought. Beat her up in broad daylight? Hardly. There were people up and down the street.

The Escort sounded its horn. There were four boys in it, two in the front and two in the back. All but the driver leant out, shouting at her again. She couldn't make out all the words, but their intention was clear enough. She stepped back as the car came crashing towards her, mounting the pavement, making her throw herself out of its path.

The next thing Clare knew she was on the ground. Her shoulder ached where she had flung herself against someone's garden wall. The Escort was beside her, both its left-side doors open. They were going to come for her. They were going to get her ... she tried to get up, and failed. She didn't care if there were four of them. She was going to fight.

But they didn't get out of the car. Instead, they leant forward and spat at her.

"Next time," said the one in the front passenger seat, "we'll run you over, or worse. That was just a warning ..."

He finished the sentence with a torrent of obscenities. Then, still sounding its horn, the car drove off, leaving Clare stranded on the pavement. Ignored by passers-by, she forced herself up, using the garden wall as a support.

4

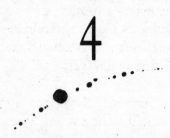

Slowly, painfully, Clare walked home. She felt dirty, defiled. She wouldn't tell Mum and Dad what had happened. Not on a day like today. But she had to tell someone. Suppose – just suppose – those four had had something to do with what happened to Angelo?

Clare threw the paper on the table and went upstairs for a shower. Undressing, she found a bright red bruise on her shoulder where she'd hit the wall. Hot water soothed the ache but not the anger. She tried to remember the faces of the boys in the car. Not one of them looked old enough to drive. Downstairs, the doorbell rang.

Mum came upstairs as Clare left the bathroom.

"Are you all right, Clare? You shot up those stairs like an alley cat when you came in."

"I'm OK, Mum."

"There's a policeman downstairs – the one who was at the hospital. He wants to ask us some questions."

Clare remembered the policeman from the hospital – a lanky, nervous youth.

"I'll be as quick as I can," she told her mum.

"And another thing . . ." Mum hesitated. "You're going to think this sounds silly . . ."

"What?"

"You know how old fashioned some of the family are. It would be best if you wore black."

"I've been wearing black jeans."

"Not jeans – a dress."

Clare couldn't believe this. Exasperated, she replied: "Mum, the only black dress I've got is the short cocktail one. I can't wear that."

"No," Mum said, patiently, "the long one. That's still in your wardrobe."

"I haven't worn that since I was fifteen!"

"You're exaggerating. Put it on – for your father – please."

Clare gave in.

"If you insist."

Mum was right. The satin dress was still there, at the back of the wardrobe, with the rest of the clothes that she hadn't taken to university. Reluctantly, Clare put it on. Then she sat in front of the mirror and brushed her hair.

Four years ago, when she and Mum bought this dress, black was the height of fashion. Then, the dress seemed daringly low cut. Now it looked modest, if a little tight. Clare had put on weight around the shoulders and thighs. She wished she'd inherited her mum's small build rather than her dad's big bones. Then she felt angry at herself. She shouldn't be thinking about her weight on a day like today. Clare went downstairs to meet the policeman.

She could hear Dad's voice booming before she got inside the room.

"Angelo . . . enemies? That's ridiculous! He was only fourteen years old."

"It's just a routine question, Mr Coppola. We have to explore every—"

"Here's Clare," Nick Coppola announced. "Tell Constable Foster, Clare. Angelo had no enemies."

The constable was sinking into one of the huge old armchairs. He looked at Clare nervously, apologetically. His shirt, Clare noticed, wasn't tucked properly into his trousers.

"None that I know of," Clare said slowly. "But I've been away at university for a year."

"Do you know who his friends at school were?" the constable asked.

Clare shook her head.

"We did go to the same secondary school: Greencoat. But Angelo started the term after I left to go to Sixth Form College."

"Did he ever talk to you about things he was interested in?"

"The usual stuff – football, computer games, videos . . ."

She hesitated and the constable made another suggestion.

"Did he talk about cars, for instance?"

"He was more interested in cycling," Dad interrupted. "He'd passed his cycling proficiency test, did I tell you that? Not that it helped him yesterday."

"Cars?" Clare returned to the subject. "How do you mean?"

Constable Foster shuffled in his armchair.

"A lot of boys round here get involved in taking without the owner's consent – that is, someone breaks into a car and then they take turns at driving it. It's what the media call 'joyriding'. Did Angelo ever mention anything like that?"

"That's ridiculous!" Dad said, angrily. "Angelo was a good boy. Never in any trouble."

Mum hushed him this time. Clare shrugged.

"He never mentioned anything like that," she said. "But then, even if he knew anything about it, I can't see him discussing it at home, can you?"

There were a few more general questions about school and Angelo's friends, then the interview was over. Clare insisted on showing the policeman out.

"Look," she said, "Constable . . ."

"Please, call me Neil," the tall youth said, awkwardly.

"Neil. Something happened to me an hour ago. There were these boys, in a yellow car, driving really fast on Churchfield Lane . . ."

Quickly, she told him the story. Neil Foster made some notes.

"Do you want to press charges against these lads?"

"No, no," Clare insisted. "And I don't want to worry my parents with it. But I thought they might be some of those joyriders you were talking about. They could have been the ones that ran over Angelo."

Neil nodded slowly.

"I'll look into it – see if what you've given me matches a stolen car – though they'll probably have dumped it by now. I might need you to drop into the station later to look at some photographs."

"OK," Clare said. "Anything you want."

Neil opened the door. He held out his hand. Clare shook it.

"Thanks for your help," he said. "I know what a hard time this must be for you."

"What were you talking to the policeman about for so long in the hallway?" Dad wanted to know.

"Not much," Clare replied. "He was just being sympathetic."

Dad frowned. Luckily, the phone rang, so Clare

went to answer it before Dad could question her further. It was her Great-Uncle Angelo, calling from Bedford. Clare brought Dad to the phone.

"No need to tell me why the young policeman was chatting to you," Mum said, when they were alone in the front room.

"How do you mean?" Clare asked, thinking she'd been overheard.

"I saw the way he was looking at you."

"Oh, Mum, don't be disgusting."

"There's nothing disgusting about being admired. But maybe you were right – that dress *is* a mistake. We'd better get you something else."

"Nothing," Neil Foster was saying to Jan Hunt in the incident room later that afternoon. "Just an ordinary lad who happened to be half Italian, who happened to be in a hit and run. What did you get?"

"Not a lot. Every time we get a witness who seems definite about something we get another who contradicts them."

Neil looked at the board. There had been fourteen witness interviews. A chart showed how they matched up.

Colour of car: green 3, yellow 4, red 1, "light" 2, "metallic" 2, don't know 2.
Number of occupants: one 6, two 2, more than two 2, "didn't see" 4.

Type of car: estate 2, large 5, hatchback 1, Volvo 1, Ford Escort 2, "foreign" 3.
Sex of driver: male 5, female 2, "didn't see" 7.
Description of driver: white 6, black 1, middle aged 2, young 2, wearing bright headband 2, underage 1.

"All we can say," Neil summed up, "is that it was probably a single white male driving a light-coloured car of average size or above. We don't even know for sure whether the car turned right from Alfreton Road, or cut across four lanes of traffic from Churchfield Lane. The witness reports are conflicting on that, too."

He drew the sketch which the Reporting Officer was obliged to fill in.

Inspector Thompson looked at the board and the sketch. Then he asked Neil about his interview with the Coppolas. Neil told him what he'd told Jan.

"That's the lot?"

"There was one other thing, sir. Probably not relevant."

"Yes?"

"The daughter, Clare – she's nineteen, a university student. It seems she had a run-in with some joyriders this afternoon. Tried to knock her over."

Thompson frowned.

"Did they say anything to her?"

"No. It sounded like some of the usual lads

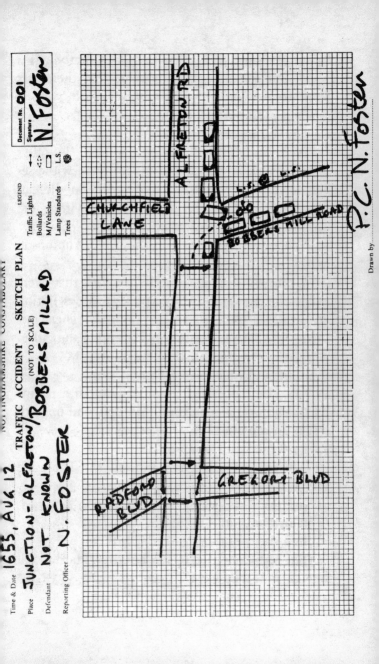

Time & Date ... 1655, AUG 12   NOTTINGHAMSHIRE CONSTABULARY

TRAFFIC ACCIDENT - SKETCH PLAN

(NOT TO SCALE)

Place ... JUNCTION - ALFRETON / BOBBERS MILL RD

Defendant ... NOT KNOWN   N. FOSTER

Reporting Officer ... N. FOSTER

LEGEND

Traffic Lights ... ⟷
Bollards ... ▭
M/Vehicles ... ▭
Lamp Standards ... L.S. ●
Trees ... ●

Document No. 001

Signature ... N. Foster

CHURCHFIELD LANE

ALFRETON RD

L.F. ● L.F.

BOBBERS MILL ROAD

RADFORD BLVD

GREGORY BLVD

Drawn by ... P.C. N. Foster

messing about, sir. Trying to give a pretty girl a scare. But she thought it possible that there was some connection with her brother's death."

Thompson didn't look impressed.

"Do you agree with her?"

"Not really," Neil had to admit. "Joyriders usually work in packs, and most of the witnesses agree that there was only one person in the car. Though I see from the chart that one witness did say the driver was underage."

"What do you want to do about it?" Thompson asked.

"I thought I might check the cars that were stolen this afternoon – I've got a good description and a partial plate from Clare Coppola. Then, if it turns out that the car was nicked, bring the girl in and get her to look at some mugshots."

Jan began to moan.

"Oh, come on, Neil. Joyriders are ten a penny. Even if you get a conviction they only end up with a slap on the wrist."

She turned to Thompson.

"This is a manslaughter enquiry, sir. There are lots of better ways of getting results."

Neil felt like kicking her. Thompson frowned, thinking about it.

"You say they threatened the girl?"

"She says they tried to run her over. Hard to tell how serious they were."

"Well, none of our other lines of enquiry seem to be getting anywhere. I'll let you spend tomorrow on it. Oh, and . . . Sergeant Hunt?"

Jan looked up.

"Sir?"

"You may be right about this being a manslaughter investigation, but we haven't yet ruled out the possibility of murder. Two of the witnesses say that the car seemed to be driving *at* the Coppola boy."

Jan gave him a disbelieving look.

"You don't—"

"There's an old Italian custom that you might have heard of: the vendetta. Yesterday, the boy; today, the girl. Keep it in mind, eh?"

He walked off, leaving Jan fuming.

" '*There's an old Italian custom you might have heard of.*' He talks like he's in a spaghetti western. You don't really buy any of that do you, Neil?"

Neil shook his head.

"Lots of easier ways to kill someone."

"So why do you want to follow this thing up with the girl?"

Neil shrugged.

"She told me about it. I said I'd check it out."

Jan gave him a sly smile.

"Good looking, is she?"

Neil tried to sound casual. He hoped his face hadn't gone red.

"Gorgeous. Like Sophia Loren must have looked when she was a teenager. But that's got nothing to do with it."

Jan gave him a sceptical look.

"If you say so. But bear this in mind. We've only got two, three days at the most before this investigation gets put on a back burner. You've just committed your morning to chasing up joyriders and you're doing overtime at the inquest for most of the afternoon. So that's a wasted day in prospect. G'night."

Neil waited until she'd gone, then picked up the phone. The information he wanted took less than five minutes to get hold of.

"The car you describe was taken from the car park of a leisure centre in West Bridgford at around two this afternoon. It hasn't been recovered yet. Do you have anything for us?"

"It was seen in Radford about an hour later," Neil replied. "I have a witness. There might be a connection with a case I'm working on. All right with you if I interview her and get back to you?"

"Might as well leave it until the morning," Neil was told. "Car should have been found by then. Ninety-nine out of a hundred are."

Neil arranged to get photos of frequent young offenders to show Clare Coppola the next day. They made depressing reading. Some of these lads had been caught ten times before they were old enough to get a provisional licence.

You got kids of fifteen who claimed to be "addicted" to driving, the same way some kids were hooked on slot machines. It was rubbish as far as Neil was concerned: these kids had dull, drab lives and all they were "addicted" to was anything that gave them a cheap thrill. You could feel sorry for them – until it was your car they took, or your brother they ran over.

He could call in on Clare Coppola on the way home, give her the news that she'd got it right about the joyriders, arrange for her to come in the next morning. Or he could talk to her on the phone. But he would like to see her again.

That stuff he'd said to Jan about Sophia Loren wasn't quite true. Clare's nose was slightly too big and her cleavage was more modest than the film star's. But there was something arresting, almost aristocratic about Clare. She had deep blue eyes with a sad, faraway look in them which wasn't just to do with her brother's death. Since the interview that afternoon, Neil had found it hard to keep her out of his mind.

He checked his watch. Going on for ten. On the late side. Tomorrow he moved from a late to an early shift, with only eight hours' sleeping time in between. He'd better go home. It would be wrong, too, to intrude on the Coppola grief for the second time in a day. A phone call would have to do. He looked up her number in the book.

"Hello?"

The voice was slightly breathy, somewhat formal. She sounded like she'd been answering the phone all day.

"Clare, this is Neil Foster at Radford Road Police Station."

"Oh, yes. Can I help you?"

"You were right about that car this afternoon. It had just been stolen."

"Really?"

She sounded excited for a moment, then her voice calmed down.

"Do you think there's any connection with—"

Neil tried to sound mature, responsible.

"I don't know. It's possible. I've been given the go-ahead to spend tomorrow morning having a look at it. Do you think you could come into the station and have a look at some photographs for me?"

"Sure." She hesitated, then added, "It'll give me an excuse to get out of the house. What time do you want me?"

"Is ten OK?"

"Ten. I'll see you then. 'Bye."

She hung up. Neil put down the phone with a big smile. As he got into his car to go home, he had to remind himself that this was an investigation into a death. Clare Coppola wouldn't be thinking about romance at all. Neither should he.

5

It was awkward, explaining to Mum and Dad why Neil Foster wanted to see her.

"He has some photographs he wants me to look at."

"Doesn't he want us to see them, too?"

"You wouldn't recognize them – kids Angelo might have known at school."

"But you weren't at school at the same time as Angelo."

"I know – it's probably a waste of time."

Clare walked to the police station. Normally, she would have used her bicycle, but times weren't normal. Should she have told Mum and Dad the truth about the joyriders? Sometimes it seemed she spent half her time avoiding telling her parents what she was really doing. Dad could blow his top at the slightest provocation. Mum would try to calm him down, but Dad always held sway.

Clare kept quiet about her boyfriends at home. Once she'd dated a boy who was Italian–English, like herself, and made the mistake of telling Dad. He tried to insist on a chaperone. Mum put a stop to that. She pointed out that Dad had married a Nottingham girl and his daughter was a Nottingham girl, too. Dad backed down. Clare learned that it was safest not to mention the boys she was seeing.

University was the other big conflict. Dad wanted her to have a *liceo classico* – a classical education, preferably studying Latin or Greek. But they didn't teach those subjects at Greencoat. Architecture was the nearest discipline to her parents' ideals that Clare could find. Even then, Dad warned Clare that it would be years and years before she earned real money, and he was aware from his position as a builder that the country was full of unemployed architects. But he was proud of Clare because she was getting the education he'd missed. Also, in a way, she was following the family tradition. Dad used to joke that he and Angelo would build the houses Clare designed.

It was another baking hot day. By the time Clare arrived at the Radford Road Police Station, sweat was trickling down the back of her grey cotton dress. She had the matching jacket draped over her shoulder for wearing later. However, it looked like she would have to change again before going to the inquest that afternoon. All this heat used up clothes.

She had to wait only a few seconds for Neil Foster. He appeared from a side door, in his shirt sleeves.

"I appreciate your coming in at a time like this. It won't take long."

He offered her coffee or a soft drink. Clare accepted lemonade. She looked around. The police station had been built only a few years ago. It didn't have the shabby look that Clare associated with such buildings. The anonymous, small rooms reminded her more of a portakabin. She'd worked in one during a placement for the architects on one of Dad's construction jobs last summer.

Neil set out the photographs.

"Take your time," he told her. "Look for as long as you want."

The pile was huge.

"It's hard to believe there are so many criminals under the age of seventeen," Clare said.

"These are just the ones associated with taking without consent," Neil told her. "Actually, the majority of petty crime in this country is committed by kids of fifteen or under. Makes you think, doesn't it?"

In the black-and-white photographs in front of Clare, everybody *looked* like a criminal. It occurred to her that if there was a photograph of Angelo here, he would look like a criminal, too. It was the guilty, suspicious way they looked at the camera. The pictured boys knew that they were being entered into a gallery of the damned.

"I only saw one of them clearly," she told Neil. "I half saw another one. It's difficult."

"Take your time."

It was tempting to pick out faces which loosely resembled those of the boys she'd seen. However, Clare was aware of the responsibility involved. Anyone she pointed out would be picked up and interviewed about his whereabouts on the previous afternoon. She had to get it right.

The other strange thing was that, now and then, she recognized someone she vaguely knew. There was a skinhead boy who lived down the street from her, and another with red hair looked like a kid at her old school. How many cars had they stolen? Every so often, she commented on one of the faces in front of her, but only to emphasize that it wasn't quite right.

"His face was a little longer than that. The hair and the eyes are right, but the jaw is wrong."

"It's no use," she said, when she'd gone through all the photographs for a second time. "They're not here. Or, if they are, I don't recognize them."

"Don't worry," said Neil. "I'd like to you try something else."

He left the room. When he returned, he was wheeling in a trolley, on which was a video recorder and a TV set.

"Some of these people don't appear on photographs," he explained. "They're too recent or they haven't been convicted yet."

The videos were taken in the entrances of police stations throughout the city, as suspects were brought in past the security camera behind the front desk.

"It runs all the time," Neil told her. "You'd be surprised how many incidents there are in the waiting areas. It's worth its weight in gold."

The quality of the pictures wasn't very good and the editing was crude. A date appeared at the bottom of the screen, beginning with January the first and slowly moving forward, day by day. As soon as a suspect had been in front of the camera long enough to be identified, the image cut to the next one.

The people in the video pictures were sadder than the ones in the photographs. You saw their whole bodies – slumped, defeated, most of them. Others tried to look jaunty, like rock musicians affecting rebellion. Many had a dazed look in their eyes which Clare assumed meant that they were on drugs.

"Just tell me if you want me to rewind any of them," Neil said.

Clare shook her head. The tapes went on and on – a badly lit video with no soundtrack, nothing to hold your interest. Some of these people are probably innocent, she told herself. But none of them *looked* innocent. Innocence didn't belong here.

"I've seen so many faces," she told Neil, "I'm not sure that even if I saw him now I'd recognize him – you know what I mean? I might end up identifying one of the people from the photographs you showed me earlier."

"We can stop if you want," Neil told her. "Take a break."

Clare looked at her watch.

"I've got to be at the inquest this afternoon. I need to go home and change."

"You look fine as you are."

Clare gave him half a smile. The fan had kept the room cool, it was true. She no longer felt dishevelled.

"I could give you a lift to the inquest."

Clare thought. If Neil drove her there, she wouldn't get sweaty again, walking home.

"OK," she said. "Can I ring my mum before we continue?"

The tapes ran for another half an hour. Slowly, the date at the bottom of the screen edged into July, then August.

"Nearly over," said Neil, unnecessarily. "We

should have time for a spot of lunch before we go to see the coroner."

Mention of lunch made Clare's stomach rumble. She hadn't eaten breakfast. No one at home had. They acted as though it was impolite to eat in the face of death.

Her mind was wandering. Clare was convinced now that the boys she had seen would not appear, that she was wasting her time. Her thoughts were moving forward to the inquest and after, to the relatives who would be arriving from Italy for the funeral. When her assailant appeared, she almost missed it.

"Wind that one back, would you?" she said to Neil.

He did it without comment. On the screen a wiry, angry-looking boy walked into a police station, this station, with his head held high.

"That's him!" Clare announced. "The driver."

"You're sure?"

"I'm positive."

Neil freeze-framed the boy's image, then checked the date at the bottom of the picture.

"I just have to make a phone call," he explained. "Watch the rest of the video while I'm gone. You might see the others."

The other boys weren't there. Neil returned to the room five minutes later.

"I've got his name," he told Clare. "We'll pick

him up later. You may have to ID him at an identification parade to establish that it was definitely him yesterday."

"It's not yesterday I'm bothered about," Clare told Neil, "it's the day before. When you interview him, you will find out what he was doing when Angelo was killed?"

"Of course." Neil smiled and opened the door. "Now, shall we get some lunch?"

Where did you take a girl like Clare Coppola? They had only half an hour, so Neil settled on the Playhouse Bar, a short walk from the coroner's offices on East Circus Street. Clare drank orange juice and wolfed down her cheese cob in seconds, so he bought her another.

While Clare ate, Neil tried to think of things to say to her. He'd never been much good at small talk. He found it hard to get beyond the football scores and station gossip. When in doubt, the other blokes at Ryton training college used to say, ask them about themselves, show them that you're really interested in *them*.

"Clare's not an Italian name, is it?"

Clare swallowed the last morsel of bread and wiped her lips before replying.

"Not a very common one. But my mum's English, as you must have noticed."

She said this in a slightly teasing way, as though

he was being a bit thick.

"But your brother was called Angelo . . ."

Clare nodded her head slowly.

"It's an old family name. My Uncle – Great-Uncle, really – Angelo gave Dad his start in the building trade over here. Mum and Dad had an agreement – Mum got to choose the name if I was a girl, Dad did if I was a boy. If the agreement had been the other way round I suppose my name would have been Angela."

She looked a little uncomfortable, discussing her dead brother. Neil quickly began asking her about university. It turned out that Clare was studying architecture, so he got her talking about buildings she liked. He acted interested, but inside he was depressed. It was obvious that Clare Coppola was out of his league. He guessed that she had a boyfriend, too, back in Manchester. But he couldn't work out how to get that information out of her.

"We'd better get going," Clare said, finally. "The inquest's in ten minutes."

Technically, Neil was off duty at two, so he could claim some overtime for his court appearance, which was good news. The couple walked to the coroner's together. Once they got inside the building, Clare put on the grey linen jacket which matched her dress. Then she brushed her black hair back over her shoulders. This more formal look seemed to age her by about five years. Neil followed her into the court at a distance. For the first time, he remembered that he had to give evidence himself, and became nervous.

When he was called, it was less stressful than other court appearances he'd made. Then, he'd always been for the prosecution. Here, no one was trying to catch him out. The only pressure on him was performing in front of Clare. He tried to avoid looking at her, as she sat between her mother and father on the front row. Behind them were several other family members and a couple of journalists.

"I held him in my arms," Neil said quietly. "He was conscious at that point. He said one word to me – 'blaze'."

"You're quite sure that was the word he used?" the coroner asked.

"Positive. It was very clear. Then he passed out."

"And what happened after that?"

"I attempted mouth-to-mouth resuscitation several times, until the ambulance came."

"And he was alive at that point?"

"He was breathing spasmodically, yes."

"But he did not regain consciousness?"

"No."

The coroner congratulated Neil on his evidence and on his exemplary conduct. Then came the medical evidence. The surgeon explained that the immediate cause of death was the chest injuries.

"But he also sustained severe injuries to the head which made his recovery extremely unlikely."

The pathologist expanded on this.

"I found brain damage of such an extent that Angelo would never have recovered full consciousness. He was almost certainly brain dead before he reached the hospital."

She was asked about the speed of the car which had hit him.

"His injuries were consistent with being hit by a motor vehicle travelling at between forty-five and fifty miles per hour."

The traffic accident investigation officer confirmed the pathologist's estimate of the car's speed. Photographs of the scene were shown. It all went very quickly.

The coroner recorded a verdict of death by misadventure and it was all over. The whole process had taken less than twenty minutes. Maria Coppola thanked Neil again on their way out. Clare didn't talk to Neil. She was busy calming down her father.

"It wasn't 'death by misadventure'," Nick Coppola was saying to a TV camera. "It was murder. And someone has to pay!"

6

"His name's Mark Crowston," Neil told Clare on the phone. "No criminal record, but his name's come up twice in connection with TWOC offences."

"*Twock?*"

"Taking without the owner's consent. Seems that Crowston's a dab hand at boosting cars."

"Should you be telling me this?" Clare asked. "I thought you said that there might be an identity parade."

"There's no point, I'm afraid," Neil said. "He admits having an altercation with you. He denies trying to run into you – naturally – and he has three witnesses who were in the car with him. They'll swear that you made abusive gestures and used foul language for no reason at all. He's lying, of course, but there are four of them against one of you."

"But the car was stolen. Surely—"

On the other end of the phone, Neil's voice became even more apologetic.

"We can't prove that, I'm afraid. Crowston claims that he was driving his brother-in-law's car, which is a similar make and colour. We've found the stolen car whose plates you gave us. But it had been burnt out on the Bestwood Estate. The fire removed the prints. Your evidence isn't enough to tie Crowston to it."

Clare was getting exasperated.

"But what about Tuesday? Couldn't that have been one of them?"

"I'm afraid Crowston has an impeccable alibi," Neil told her. "He and two of the other lads in the car were in court, charged with two TWOC offences from back in the spring. They got off. That was why they were out joyriding yesterday. They were celebrating."

"What about the fourth one?"

"He couldn't have done it either, I'm afraid."

"Why?"

"He's broken his right arm."

Clare wanted to scream.

"We'll get them in the end," Neil told her. "Crowston's already been arrested again for another offence. That was why he was on the video you saw."

Neil was trying to make his voice soothing, to calm her down. Clare hated it when people treated her that way. As far as she was concerned, the conversation was over. Neil Foster, however, kept talking.

"How are you keeping?" he asked.

"I'm OK. I'll be glad when the funeral's over."

"That's not 'til Monday, is it?"

"That's right."

"I was thinking . . ."

"Yes?"

Neil's voice stumbled over the words.

"I've got the weekend off. I thought you might want to do something to take your mind off things – go to the pictures or something like that."

Clare waited for him to finish, but Neil clearly thought he had made himself clear.

"You mean, with you?" Clare prompted.

He laughed nervously.

"Yes. Sorry. Didn't I say that?"

Clare took a deep breath. She was used to dealing with boys asking her out, but not in circumstances like this.

"It's very nice of you, Neil. But I've got loads of relatives arriving this weekend and I'm expected to be here. You know how it is."

"Sure. Another time, maybe."

"Maybe, yes. Thanks for asking. 'Bye."

She put the phone down before he could say anything else. It was supposed to be flattering when someone asked you out, but Clare usually found it embarrassing. She had been thinking of Neil as a police officer, not a potential boyfriend. Men should be able to tell if you liked them, then they wouldn't risk the humiliation of being turned down. But most of the men she met seemed to know less about women than they did about modern architecture. Which was nothing at all.

"Neil, I don't want to be funny, but . . ."

"What?"

"I couldn't help overhearing your conversation with the Coppola girl."

Neil blushed. He thought Jan was going to tease him about asking her out. She wasn't.

"What about it?"

"You were giving her information which wasn't necessary – the guy's name for a start, not to mention his alibi. You're only meant to tell her what's pertinent to her involvement in the investigation."

"Oh, come on, Sarge. What possible harm—"

Neil called Jan "Sarge" only when he was annoyed with her.

"I'm just warning you, that's all. Suppose some of her friends were to find out where Crowston lives, harass him . . ."

Neil laughed.

"You're almost as bad as the Inspector, with all that 'vendetta' nonsense."

"And you're as bad as all the rest, giving the girl special treatment because you fancy her!"

Neil came over and put his hand on Jan's shoulder. Jan hated it when coppers behaved in that patronizing way, particularly when they were younger than her.

"You're over-reacting," Neil said. "He was in court. It's a matter of public record."

"All right," said Jan, shaking off his hand. "So now you can give me some help. I persuaded the boss to let me check out that car model angle, the one you were so keen on, but I can't work out how to access it on the computer. Give me a hand, would you?"

Neil grinned.

"Not entirely computer literate, are we?"

Jan gritted her teeth.

"I know how to use the system, but not for this. And your training is a lot more recent than mine. The programs change constantly, don't they?"

Neil nodded.

"Yeah, well I've had a load of 'hands-on' experience, it's true . . ."

Jan flinched. She'd had enough weak sexist jokes to last her a lifetime. She knew all the put-down replies, but was getting tired of using them.

"I know the only thing you've had your hands on, my lad."

Water off a duck's back. Neil didn't even bother replying. He was busy playing with the keyboard. Two minutes later, he pressed the button marked "print" and paper began to spew out of the bubble jet. Smart alec!

"I can't access the cars with 'blaze' in the model name," he told Jan. "The computer doesn't allow that. So I'm getting a printout of all the different types of cars and model names, going back ten years. We can go through them manually."

He meant by looking at them.

"How long will that take?"

"Not long."

The printout was on its third sheet. Jan looked at it. The list was only halfway through the Alfa Romeos. She handed it to Neil.

"Not long, huh?"

He frowned, then gave her another of his silly grins.

"Good thing you've got me here to help you."

Clare's grandmother arrived on Saturday afternoon, along with two of her uncles and her Aunt Rafaella. Clare hadn't seen any of the Italian side of the family since she last visited their village, two years before. She accompanied Dad as he drove down to meet them. They didn't talk much on the way, but spent the entire journey listening to classical music on Radio Three, each engrossed in their own thoughts.

The reunion at the airport was sombre. Only Uncle Roberto spoke to her in English.

"You look wonderful, Clare."

She was wearing the new black dress Mum had bought her in Jessops, after the inquest. Roberto went on.

"Like your Aunt Rafaella did when she was your age – a real beauty."

Clare let the rest of the conversation wash over her. Her Italian wasn't too strong, but she caught the general drift, which was the same as everybody had been saying for the last five days – it was a tragedy, a terrible waste, and something dreadful should be done to the villain responsible.

Once they got home, the atmosphere was claustrophobic. The house was too full. Her uncles shared Angelo's bedroom and Grandma had the spare. Rafaella shared with Clare. On Sunday morning, it was impossible to get into the bathroom before church. When they got back, Uncle Angelo and three more Coppolas had arrived. Since only Roberto spoke much English, most of the conversation was in Italian. Clare joined her mum in the kitchen. Maria was upset.

"You know, when I was pregnant with Angelo,

before Nick started the business, he had a chance of a job back home in the village. He tried to persuade me to go back with him. We'd have less money, he said, but we'd be happier. The village was a good place to bring children up. And I . . . and I . . ."

She was on the verge of tears. Clare held her hand.

"I said no. I don't remember what reasons I gave Nick. He didn't press me. Both of my parents were still alive then. It was the end of the seventies and unemployment was just starting to get high. We could see that things were going to get worse, but I thought Italy wouldn't be any better. I hardly spoke the language and your dad's family frightened me a little. They were all older than me. They didn't really approve of Nick marrying an English girl. Yet now . . ."

Tears were streaming down Mum's face, but she didn't dry them.

"Now they've all come over to grieve for Angelo. And they're all warm, loving people who've borrowed money to get the air fare and I think – if I'd gone over there, this wouldn't have happened. Angelo would be alive, with all his relatives around him. We'd be happy. Instead . . ."

She broke down. Clare hugged her.

"You can't change the past, Mum. No one can say what would have happened if we'd lived in

Italy. I'm not sure if I'd have been as happy as I have been, but that isn't the point. What's done is done. Please stop crying."

Mum shook her head as her tears soaked into Clare's dress.

"No. I need to cry. It helps."

Clare was crying, too. She was dimly aware of people looking into the kitchen, then moving quickly away, allowing them to grieve with dignity. After another minute, Mum broke away from Clare.

"Thank you," she said. "I needed to do that."

She washed her face in the sink. Clare wiped her own eyes.

"Will you be all right now?" she asked.

Mum nodded.

"I'd better go and talk to your aunt and uncles. What are you going to do?"

"I really need to get out of the house for a while," Clare told her. "There's some kind of festival on at the Forest, with music and stuff. I think I might walk over there and have a look."

"Go on," Mum said. "Get going. There's only your dad'll notice. I'll square it with him."

Clare changed into jeans and a light T-shirt. It was a great relief to get out of the house and its stifling atmosphere. She walked over to the Forest recreation ground. The Rock and Reggae Festival was held there, on the large grassy area where Nottingham Forest, the football team, used to play. It was a free festival. Every year the Council threatened to close it down because of noise, or damage or drugs or something. Yet, somehow, it always survived.

The afternoon was at its hottest, and there was a pleasant lethargy about the festival. Children played on the grass. Many of them had had their faces painted at one of the stalls. Exotically dressed people were picnicking on the grass, enjoying the rough and ready music.

Two hundred metres away, on Sherwood Rise, was the Italian Community Centre. It might as well be on another planet. Here, unkempt crusties played thrash metal on the main stage. The latest rave sounds came from one of the marquees. There were a few police around, in their shirt sleeves, maintaining a low profile. It was a relaxing place to be.

However, after an hour, Clare had looked at enough stalls selling trinkets and tapes and the music bored her. She wasn't ready to go home, so she decided to walk up the hill to the tree-lined slopes of the upper part of the Forest.

A road ran across the middle, separating one half from the other. Beyond it, on the left, was an old graveyard, long full up. Clare walked there sometimes, on her own. In the middle was a vast hollow where the city's paupers used to be buried. It would be cool there. Clare decided that she needed to walk around for a while, to spend some time thinking about Angelo.

The entrance was on the main road. Clare left the festival, passed the all-weather soccer pitch and joined the slip road that led onto the Mansfield Road. Cars were coming down the slip road and parking in order to visit the festival, although they weren't supposed to stop there. Clare hardly paid any attention to them. She didn't look back, even when one of them slowed to a crawl behind her.

The front of the car nudged Clare's left buttock and she spun around.

"What do you think you're playing at?" she yelled.

The car stopped and the driver got out. It was the youth she'd identified two days before: Mark Crowston.

"You and I need to have a talk," he said.

Clare stood her ground.

"We've got nothing to talk about," she told the ugly youth.

His hair was cut shorter than it had been on the video. He wore a torn T-shirt. His three side-kicks were in the car, leering at her through the windows.

"She looks a bit tasty today," one of them called. "Why don't we take her for a ride?"

Clare flinched.

"Leave me alone," she said loudly. "I don't want anything to do with you."

She turned on her heel, intending to walk off. Crowston grabbed her shoulder. The other youths got out of the car, blocking her path.

"You went to see the police about us, didn't you?" Crowston sneered. "That wasn't a very nice thing to do, was it?"

Clare was silent. Crowston continued.

"A little bird told me that your brother got run over. What a shame."

Anger replaced fear. Clare was livid. She slapped Crowston hard on the face.

"You—"

Stung by the pain, Crowston let go of her for a moment. Clare seized her chance. She ran between Crowston's henchmen, up the hill.

Immediately, she knew she'd made a mistake. She should have headed downwards, towards the safety of the festival crowd. The hill was steep and the joyriders were taller than her, would run faster. Already she could hear them getting nearer and nearer. She had only one advantage over them. She knew her way around the graveyard and they probably didn't. But first she had to get in there.

Clare charged into the cemetery and took the path that ran diagonally across the centre, through the gravestones. The yobs were advancing on her.

She had to put them off. Gasping for breath, she ducked between a white, crumbling sepulchre and a grassy, unmarked mound. The four youths ran past her.

On her left was the path which led down to the paupers' graves. She might be able to hide there, but if these boys found her, she'd be trapped. She decided to double back on herself and get out of the cemetery. She joined the path and began to run. A high wall hid her from watching eyes, then dipped again. Suddenly, she could see two of them. And they could see her.

"There she is!"

They were on the same path, running straight towards her. Clare made for the path she'd just run down. But there, at the other end of it, were the other two. She froze, not knowing what to do. The only way she could go now was down into the huge hollow where the paupers were buried. But if she ran down there, she would be trapped. There was only one thing for it. She would have to try to scale the wall to her right, then jump over the other side.

Quickly, Clare jumped onto the sandstone wall, at a point where it was only a little taller than she was. She was wearing trainers, and managed to get some purchase with her feet. She looked over the edge of the wall, knowing that the drop on the other side was going to be bigger than the one she'd just climbed. It was at least five metres. She could easily break something. But she had to try. Behind her, she heard Crowston's voice.

"We'll have her now!"

Clare tried to swing her body over the wall, but it was no good. A rough hand grabbed her foot.

"Gotcha!"

The sandstone crumbled away at her feet and she fell to the stone floor, knocking her ankle.

"No!" she screamed.

She heard a loud, piercing whistle coming from behind her. Crowston yelled, "You asked for this!"

Clare looked up to see a large boot heading directly for her face.

7

In the end Jan brought the work home with her. Kevin hated it when she did that. He said her weekends off were for them. He would never let Jan pull overtime when Forest were playing at home, even though sometimes they could do with the money. Especially, as it turned out, now.

The printout was a hundred and two pages long. Jan was on page ninety-two. In ten minutes, she would have found out if a car with the model name "Blaze" had been sold new in Great Britain during the last ten years.

"Jan!"

Kevin had come in from his game of badminton. He walked into the living room, leant over her armchair, and kissed her on the neck. His hair was still wet from the shower and it dripped onto her, refreshingly cool.

"You're not still doing that? You were at it when I went out."

"I know, but Mum rang up."

Kevin's eyes widened.

"Did you tell her?"

Jan's eyes met his. Let him work it out.

"You didn't tell her?"

Jan nodded.

"Wait another week. Until I'm sure."

"Whatever you say," Kevin told her. "As long as you haven't changed your mind."

Jan smiled.

"I haven't changed my mind."

Kevin grinned.

"Are you ready for the monthly ritual?"

"I told you – ten minutes."

"Leave that until tomorrow, when you're being paid to work on it."

"I'll be ready by the time you've got changed and dried your hair."

Kevin kissed her again and left the room.

The "monthly ritual" was the visit to Jan's in-laws for Sunday dinner. They were nice people, but they were boring. And they couldn't understand why their successful doctor son had married, of all things, a policewoman.

Jan's eyes moved down the page at double speed.

Once, she'd planned to make Inspector by the time she was thirty-five. It would never happen now. She moved onto the next page. Astonishing, the number of cars that Volvo made. None of them with a model name of "Blaze". The next page. More Volvos. It was going to be a Sunday roast, of course. Who wanted to eat a roast dinner when the weather was as hot as this? All Jan fancied was a salad, maybe a little shellfish. Was she allowed to eat shellfish any more? She didn't know. Another page. Another.

There was actually a car called a Yakimoto. She'd heard of Yamaha, Honda and, of course, Toyota. But Yakimoto? She'd never seen one of them. Mind you, there were only three models: the compact, Stella, which had an 1100 cc engine, the standard 1300 model, Lone Star, which sounded like it ought to be American. Then there was the souped-up 1.6 GTI version, which she had to turn the page to get the model name for: Blaze.

She read it again to make sure that she wasn't hallucinating, that it didn't read "Black" or "Blazer" or "Daze". No – there it was, at the top of the page. Jan gave a whoop.

"Got it!"

"That's good. Can we go now?"

Kevin had come back into the room wearing his plaid cotton button-down shirt. He always wore his best clothes to go to his mother's.

"In a minute," Jan said, with a smile.

"But you said you'd got it."

"I need to make sure."

There was a possibility – remote, but nevertheless a possibility – that there was another car with the model name Blaze. The secret of good police work was thoroughness. Jan was always thorough. Before carrying on, though, she read the model details again – the Yakimoto was a hatchback, which didn't tie with most of the witnesses' statements, but it came in three colours: yellow, dark green and, lastly, lime green, which did. And the speed made sense, too. It was the sort of car that people who drove fast used.

Best of all, only a tiny number of Yakimoto 1.6s had been imported to Britain, according to this report – a little over a hundred. If the car which knocked over Angelo Coppola, causing his death, was a Yakimoto Blaze, then the police had an excellent chance of catching the driver.

But just to be sure, Jan went back to the last five pages of the printout.

Clare covered her face with her arms, but the blow didn't come. Instead, she heard the loud whistle again, nearer this time. She looked up and the youths were running away.

"Next time!" Crowston yelled, as he vanished into the endless tombs.

Neil Foster, in his short-sleeved light blue shirt, came running around the corner. Clare had never been gladder to see anyone in her life.

"Are you all right?"

She tried to stand up, but stumbled. Neil caught her and held her close. Clare realized that she was shaking.

"I was so scared," she told him.

"You're all right now."

They sat down on a grassy knoll, next to what looked like a crypt.

"Was it Crowston?" Neil asked.

Clare nodded.

"They ran into me – literally – as I was leaving the festival."

"I know," Neil said. "I saw. I didn't notice you until you were leaving. Then, when I saw the lads getting out of the car, I came as quickly as I could."

"I'm glad you did."

Neil smiled. He squeezed her arm, gently.

"I'll go and see Crowston tomorrow, drag him into the station for a caution, tell him what'll happen if he comes near you again."

Clare was beginning to feel calmer. Her shoulder and her ankle ached from the fall.

"Won't it be like before?" she asked. "My word against him and his mates?"

Neil shook his head.

"I'll tell him I saw him, too."

"But you had to ask me whether it was him."

"Only you and I know that."

"Wouldn't stand up in court," Clare said.

"It doesn't have to," Neil assured her. "I just need to keep him away from you. But you'll still need to watch out. Crowston hangs around with some violent people. Have you told your family about him?"

Clare didn't answer.

"You haven't, have you?"

"No. They've got enough on their plate."

She remembered something.

"He knows about Angelo," Clare told Neil. "He made a joke about it."

"I think you ought to tell your parents," Neil said.

Clare didn't answer this.

"Would you like me to get you a car to take you home?" Neil asked.

"No, I'll be all right, really," Clare said. Then she added, more warmly, "Is that offer of a film still open?"

Neil's eyes brightened up.

"Of course."

"Everyone should be gone by Tuesday afternoon," Clare told him. "I'll need to get out of the house by the evening."

"What would you like to watch?"

"I don't know. Why don't we go down to the Showcase, see what's on?"

"Fine."

They exchanged awkward goodbyes. Clare walked home slowly, trying to ignore the pain in her leg where she'd fallen on it. She wasn't sure why she'd given Neil a date. Partly it was gratitude. He had saved her from a beating. Partly it was because he looked so eager. She knew that look. Neil was smitten with her and Clare felt bad about disappointing him. Yet also, she had to admit to herself, she was going out with Neil because she wanted to get close to the investigation into her brother's death. But there was nothing wrong with that. Was there?

"What do you want to see Crowston for?" Jan asked Neil. "I thought you'd eliminated him and his cronies."

"They had a go at Clare Coppola on Sunday afternoon."

"How do you mean, 'had a go'?"

"Chased her up the Mansfield Road to the old cemetery. I think they were going to beat her up before I got there."

"So you played the knight in shining armour, did you?"

Neil gave her a sly grin, which was rather unlike him.

"Something like that, as it turned out."

"But no offence was committed?"

"Not as such. No."

They parked the car halfway up a side road on the Whitemoor Estate. Jan knocked on the door of a dowdy semi-detached house with crumbling brickwork. It was answered by a woman of indeterminate age.

"Mrs Crowston?"

"What do you want?"

"Is Mark in?"

She gave them both hostile looks.

"What's it about?"

"We want to speak to him. Is he in, Mrs Crowston?"

"He's in bed."

"Would you get him up, please?"

It was eleven in the morning. Jan and Neil waited in the dingy, fusty-smelling front room of the house, trying not to look at the peeling wallpaper, the carpet covered in cigarette burns. They'd both spent time in much less pleasant places. Jan had been brought up in a series of them: run-down, squalid flats which her single-parent mother was always having to leave because she was behind with the rent. According to the sociologists, a background like that should make you become a criminal, not a copper. Jan didn't have a lot of time for sociologists.

Mark Crowston took five minutes to emerge from his bedroom. When he did, he was wearing ripped jeans and had a bare torso, exposing two tattoos: one was of a coiled snake; the other, almost touchingly, read "Mum". He lit a cigarette and sat down in a decrepit corduroy-backed armchair. He spoke before they did.

"I told you on Friday I had nothing to do with the Coppola kid."

"How come you know the name?" Neil asked.

Crowston sneered.

"Read the papers, don't I?"

"But that's not what we're here about," Jan told him.

Crowston squinted at them. Probably needs glasses, Jan thought. Too vain to wear them.

"Well?" Crowston asked.

He was looking at Jan. She should be dealing with this, not Neil. She was more experienced. But for Neil it was personal. So she let him get on with it.

"I saw you yesterday," Neil told Crowston.

"Oh, yeah? In the White Lion, were you?"

"No. I was patrolling the Rock and Reggae Festival, on the Forest."

Crowston laughed.

"You wouldn't see me near there – load of hippies, crusties, lousy music . . . you're kidding, right?"

Slowly, Neil shook his head.

"You didn't go into the festival itself."

"I didn't go near the festival. I told you, I was in the pub when—"

Neil leant forward.

"When *what?* I didn't tell you a time, or what happened."

Calm down, Jan wanted to tell Neil. Let him find enough rope to hang himself with.

"I was in the pub," Crowston repeated.

And Neil blew his cool.

"You were harassing a girl called Clare Coppola, whose brother died last week, and who you tried to run over the following day. There's no point in denying it, because I was there!"

Crowston shrugged.

"If you say so. What's the problem? Harassment? Big deal!"

"You also assaulted her . . ."

That wasn't what Neil had told Jan earlier. The young policeman went on.

"If I hadn't arrived, you'd have beaten her up!"

Crowston stood up.

"Says who? You reckon you saw me – there are a hundred blokes who look like me. How close were you?"

Neil didn't reply.

"You say this Coppola girl *nearly* got beaten up. So where's the crime? All I know is this girl's got a grudge against me because I drive a car the same colour as the one that killed her brother . . ."

Neil stood too, now, looking triumphant.

"How do you know what colour the car was?"

Crowston stubbed his cigarette out in the fireplace.

"Don't make me laugh."

Jan put a gentle arm on Neil's shoulder. Then she spoke to Mark Crowston, very softly, but very firmly.

"Mark Crowston, I am cautioning you for threatening behaviour towards Clare Coppola yesterday afternoon. No charges are being brought at this stage, but if there is any repetition – indeed, if you ever go near Clare Coppola again – you will be in deep trouble. Do you understand me?"

"I understand that you've got nothing on me."

"Well, then," Jan said, at the edge of her patience, "you'd better make sure that you don't give us any reason to arrest you. Because if you do, we'll throw the book at you! Got that?"

Crowston turned his back on them. Jan grabbed Neil and got him out of the house before he made more of a mess of things. Once they were in the car, she blew her top at him.

"Crowston's been avoiding the law since he was ten years old! He knows the rules better than we do. You've got to be more subtle, Neil – draw him out a bit at a time. All you did was raise his hostility – he hardly took in the warning we were there to give him."

Neil was indignant.

"What about the things he said about the colour of the car? Maybe he was out of court by the time the accident took place. Maybe he *was* driving that car."

Jan shook her head.

"He was winding us up. He doesn't know the colour of the car that killed Angelo Coppola any more than we do. By the way, was he right? Were you too far away from the incident yesterday to identify him properly?"

Neil was silent for a moment.

"It looked like him," he mumbled eventually. "Clare said it was him."

"You're impossible," Jan told him. "Let's just hope it's the last time we see that excuse for a human being."

She turned the car out of the estate, heading right, away from the station.

"Where are we going?" Neil asked.

Jan didn't reply for a while. Neil asked again. This time, she replied.

"We're going to see one of the two people in the city who own a Yakimoto 1.6," she told him.

"A what?"

"A car with the model name, 'Blaze'."

8

Brian Boland's Yakimoto Blaze was parked outside his insurance office. It was yellow. There was nothing special about the car. You'd have been hard pushed to say what separated it from at least a dozen other cars on the market.

Before going in, Neil and Jan examined the front of the car very carefully. No dents, no suspicious scratches or cracks on the bumper. Nothing which could be the consequence of a head-on collision with a cyclist. Nor were there any signs of recent bodywork which might have been done to cover up such a collision. Appearances could be deceptive, though – new work could be made to look old and some car deaths left no traces of the incident on the car itself. Not even blood.

And there was one thing: on the front left-hand wing, written in bright red letters, was what must have been the last word that Angelo Coppola ever read: *Blaze*.

Boland was in his forties and overweight. His nose had exposed veins and the mottled look which indicates a heavy drinker. He was an insurance broker.

"I often find," he told Jan and Neil, "that police officers, as a breed, are under-insured. They tend to think that it'll never happen to them, because of their jobs. Whereas you'd think, with their jobs, that they'd know the risks and take action to avoid them. Am I right or am I right?"

Neil didn't answer. He didn't have any insurance, other than for his car. Who needed it, when you lived at home with your parents?

"Take life insurance, for example. Do either of you have life insurance?"

Before Neil could answer, Jan made her point.

"We're here to talk to you about your whereabouts last week, Mr Boland."

Boland sighed. He got a packet of mints out of his pocket and offered them to each of the officers, both of whom refused. Then he popped one into his mouth. Probably used them to mask the smell of alcohol, Neil decided.

"Am I in some kind of trouble?" Boland asked, politely.

"Not at all," said Neil. "We just need to eliminate you from our enquiries."

"What enquiries?"

The phone rang. Boland reached over to pick it up, looked at Jan and Neil, then changed his mind. Instead, he pressed the button which activated the answering machine. They heard his voice saying:

"This is Brian Boland Insurance Associates. I'm afraid that we can't take your call right now, but if you . . ."

The voice cut off as the caller hung up. Boland shook his head ruefully.

"Up to fifty per cent do that, you know. Can't stand talking into a machine. If I had the—"

"Mr Boland," Neil interrupted, "can you tell us where you were on the afternoon of Tuesday last?"

"Certainly."

Boland opened a desk drawer and pulled out a filofax. He flicked to the right page and pushed it across the desk to Jan and Neil. Too casual, Neil thought. He behaved like he was used to being questioned by the police.

The diary read like this:

10.00 Drexel Ltd
11.30 Simon Harrison
12.00 Karen Black
02.00 Market

"'Market'?" Jan asked.

"The Market Club. It's just off—"

"I know where it is," Jan said.

The Market Club was an all-day drinking bar, and had been since before all-day licensing was introduced. Its clientele were mainly market traders, but also included fringe elements of the criminal fraternity. It wasn't the sort of place you'd expect to find a businessman like Boland.

"Kind of a short working day, isn't it?" Neil asked.

"I do a lot of business in the Market Club," Boland replied. "You'd be surprised."

"Life insurance?" Jan suggested.

"Yes. And other things."

"What time did you leave?" Neil said, almost casually.

"Now there's a question."

"Try to answer it, please," Jan said, without a trace of impatience.

Boland appeared to be thinking about it.

"Could have been three. Could have been four."

That was too early.

"Which?" Neil asked.

"I guess that it would be the later time," Boland said. "But I'm not sure."

"Can you give us the names of anybody there who'd remember?" Jan asked.

Boland looked shifty for a moment. He's been lying, Neil thought. We're going to get him.

"There's the barman, Dave," he said slowly.

"We'll need more than that," Jan told him, firmly. "The names of everyone you met there."

"I'm not sure I'll be able to remember," Boland said slowly. "You see, I had a few."

"Please try."

He gave them some names and Jan wrote them down. Finally, she asked, "And you're sure you don't remember what time you drove home?"

Boland frowned.

"It may have been a bit later than four," he said. "I seem to remember that the traffic was bad."

Neil felt like cheering. Wait till he told Clare Coppola about this.

"Oh, but I didn't drive," Boland added, almost as an afterthought. "Not after drinking, obviously. I caught a bus."

Ten minutes later Jan and Neil drove back to the station. According to Boland, after failing to sell some life insurance to Karen Black, he had driven to his home, where he had deposited the car, then caught the bus into town, walking from Slab Square to the Market Club.

"I suppose it saved on the parking fees," Jan said.

"You believe him?" Neil asked, incredulously.

"No," said Jan. "I don't believe him. But if you

were being interviewed by the police you wouldn't admit to drunken driving, would you? Doesn't mean he's guilty of killing Angelo Coppola."

"Makes it a darn sight more likely, though," Neil said.

"Agreed."

Neil checked the time. Twelve-thirty. Elsewhere, he knew, just a few kilometres away, Angelo Coppola was being buried.

"So who's got the other car?"

Jan checked her notes.

"A woman called Dawn Miller. We can't see her until this evening."

"This evening?" Neil groaned. "Why not?"

"Because she's in court this afternoon."

"Another one in court – what's she done?"

"Nothing, as far as I know. She's a probation officer."

Clare had been to funerals before, but never one where someone had died young. There was so much grief, and no one trying to hide it. Clare found it impossible to hold back her tears.

"It's right to cry," Aunt Rafaella said, her own eyes moist. "You cry as much as you want."

Somehow, Mum and Dad stayed in control, even when the priest delivered a eulogy to Angelo which made him sound like a saint. Perhaps he went too far. To Clare, her brother had been a normal, naughty boy, always getting in her way. Now he would never be anything else to her.

The chapel was full, not just with family. Many of Angelo's schoolfriends were there. Some of Clare's came, too: Denise, Sarah, Helen. Denise had been her best friend before she went to university. Now she was a secretary. Inevitably, they had drifted apart. Sarah and Helen both went to different universities, doing different courses. They saw each other much less than before, too. With them, though, it didn't matter so much, because they were having similar experiences.

This afternoon the four girls were as close as ever. Each of them hugged Clare in turn. It had never felt more important to have friends.

"You must come out soon," Denise said. "Take your mind off things."

The four of them arranged to go out on Wednesday. Then Clare went home to a house full of grieving relatives.

Soon everyone was eating. A feast of food was laid out – much of it more suitable, Clare thought, for a wedding than a funeral: fancy breads, pickles, salami, hams, gherkins, huge, ripe tomatoes, endless different cheeses and, on another table, an array of cakes which Clare would have found mouthwatering any other day. Today, the sight of people tucking in made her feel sick. She retreated to her usual hiding place, the kitchen, expecting to find her mum there.

Instead she found Dad, with Uncle Roberto. They were talking in Italian, but Clare could work out what was being said. Roberto was saying, "And if you find him, you know what you must do. It's a matter of honour."

"Roberto, Roberto . . ." Dad shook his head. "We're not in Italy . . ."

Then he noticed Clare, and quickly changed the subject.

Dawn Miller had told Jan that she would be home by a quarter to six, so she and Neil arrived at ten to. The door was answered immediately. Dawn was a handsome Afro-Caribbean woman about the same age as Jan. She wore a white linen suit and a plain but expensive red silk blouse.

"How come you people are only ever early when it's inconvenient?" she asked. "I haven't had time to get changed yet."

Jan apologized.

"This'll only take a few minutes," she said. "We're anxious to get home ourselves."

"Tell me about it."

Jan went through what she wanted to know. Dawn consulted her diary.

"I was in court between three and four," she told them. "Then I went back to the office. I guess that

I would have come home about five – that's the normal time."

"Do you remember the journey home?" Neil asked.

"Any reason why I should?"

This interview was totally unlike the one with Boland. Dawn Miller had nothing to hide. They were three professionals, going about their business. Nevertheless, Jan played it by the book.

"You were travelling by car?"

"That's right. Oh, hang on, that was the grid-lock day, wasn't it?"

Jan nodded.

"Yes, I remember now. I just missed it. I was listening to the reports on the radio, counting my blessings."

"How come?" Neil asked. "I mean, if you left work at five . . . the whole city was snarled up."

"But I didn't leave at five," Dawn told them. "I left just after four to visit a client, in Radford, on my way home. I left him just before five."

Jan smiled at her.

"Could you tell me the client's name?"

"Nick Shears. Male. Thirty-nine. On parole after being released halfway through a three-year sentence for drug dealing."

"And you were visiting this guy on your own?" Neil asked. "Is that usual for a female probation officer?"

"Not usual, no. But, to be honest, I wasn't expecting him to be home. He hadn't turned up for his last two visits to the office. I wanted to check that he was still at the same address."

"And he was?"

"Yes. He said he'd been ill, apologized."

"And was that all right?" Jan asked.

Dawn shrugged. Sometimes, Jan couldn't believe how soft the system was. The way she saw it, parole shouldn't exist. Someone got three years, they should serve three years. But the prisons were overcrowded, so if you kept your nose clean, you might get out after one. In theory, you would be sent straight back if you committed another crime. In theory. But Jan kept her views to herself.

"How long had he been a client?" Neil asked.

"Nearly four months. He'd served eighteen months, which meant he had to do six months on parole. He was still on weekly visits. We would have relaxed that, but then he went AWOL."

"You'd better give us his address," Jan said. "Just a formality, you understand, but we have to make sure."

Dawn shrugged, then dictated it to Jan, from memory. Jan's ears pricked up. The address was a road off Churchfield Lane, which was the road they thought the hit-and-run driver had come from.

"Which way did you drive home?" Jan asked.

Dawn thought for a moment.

"I went along Churchfield Lane, turned right onto Alfreton Road, then left along the boulevards until I got to Mansfield Road. Why? What's all this about?"

"Just routine," Neil said. "Before we go, do you mind if we take a look at your car?"

"Of course not," Dawn Miller told them. "It's in the garage."

She offered them the keys, then paused.

"You don't think I knocked over that boy, do you? Good God!"

"Just routine," Jan repeated. "Nothing at all for you to worry about."

They went out to the garage. Neil opened it. Inside was Dawn Miller's lime green Yakimoto Blaze.

"Look at that," Neil said.

Beneath the headlight was a long angular scratch, nearly two centimetres wide.

"It looks as though she bumped into something," Jan said, thoughtfully.

Neil's voice was more angry.

"It looks like she ran into the handlebars of a bike."

9

The film they chose in the end was a light comedy. Clare didn't laugh much, but it took her mind off her troubles. Afterwards, they went for a drink in the Boat Inn. Neil off-duty, in jeans and a rugby shirt, was a different, more relaxed person. Clare was surprised to realize that she quite fancied him.

"What were you doing at the Rock and Reggae Festival?" he asked. "I wouldn't have thought it was your sort of scene."

"I just needed to get out of the house," Clare told him, wondering what he thought her "scene" was. "What were you doing there, anyway? You told me you had the weekend off."

Neil shrugged.

"I did, but I had nothing special to do, so I decided to earn some overtime. I'm saving up for a house."

"Where do you live now?"

"With my mum and my younger sister, in Wollaton."

"Mmmm, Wollaton," Clare teased him. "That's quite posh."

"On the council estate behind the park."

Embarrassed, Clare quickly moved the conversation on.

"How long have you been in the police?"

"Eight months. I've just finished my foundation period."

"Tell me about the training."

Neil gave her a look, as if to see that she was really interested, not just making up for her gaffe about Wollaton. Then he told her.

"It takes two years. The first 31 weeks is the foundation period. You do ten weeks at the Regional Training school at Ryton."

"What do they teach you?"

"All sorts. Experiential learning, they call it. You do lots of role-play. How to deal with the public. How to manage stress. The law, of course, and all the different police procedures."

"Your course sounds a lot more interesting than mine. What happens next?"

"Then you do five weeks with your tutor

constable, working the area where you're going to work eventually. Then a week off, then another five weeks with your tutor and, finally, a week at Epperstone training school for what they call 'smoothing over' and final assessment."

"Which you passed?"

"Yes."

"So what happens now?"

"For the rest of the two years, I'm on my probationary period, monitored by my sergeant. I'm driving with her at the moment. Jan Hunt."

"What's she like?"

Neil smiled hesitantly.

"Jan's a good officer – very efficient. She gets a bit uptight sometimes, but nobody's perfect."

"What made you become a policeman?" Clare wanted to know.

Neil looked bashful.

"The usual reasons."

"Don't tell me – you like wearing a uniform and your favourite TV programme is *The Bill*."

Neil shook his head.

"I wanted a steady job with good money. My dad got made redundant when he was forty-five. He was on the dole for ten years before he died."

Clare was ashamed of being flippant. Other people had their troubles, too.

"I'm sorry," she said. "How long ago was that?"

"Last year," Neil told her. "Heart attack."

"Let's talk about something more cheerful."

They struck up a conversation about films and football teams. It was a bit strained. If Clare had come across Neil at university, where most of her friends were arty types, they would never have hit it off. But this was Nottingham. Here, she needed him. She didn't ask too many questions about his work. She didn't want him thinking that she was only going out with him because of her brother, even if it turned out to be true. So far, all he had told her was that Crowston had been cautioned for chasing her two days before. He wasn't allowed to discuss the ongoing investigation, he said. It was against the rules.

By their second drink, the conversation had moved on to Clare's family.

"My Uncle Angelo came over in the fifties," Clare explained. "The London Brick Company brought over whole villages from Southern Italy in those days, settled them in Bedford. In the sixties, Angelo set up his own building firm. My dad came over to work for him in the seventies. He did some jobs for people in Nottingham, met my mum, married her, and Angelo helped him to set up his own firm here."

"And your father named his firstborn son after his benefactor."

"Yes."

"Yours is small for an Italian family."

"I think Dad would have liked a huge family, like the one he comes from. But two of us was quite enough for Mum."

But now she's got none at home, Clare thought. And Dad still works all hours. How's she going to cope with all that time alone?

"Will you find him?" she asked suddenly, in a desperate voice. "Will you catch the person who killed Angelo?"

"I hope so," Neil said. "We've got a couple of good leads, which we're checking out. It should only be a matter of time."

"What kind of leads?" Clare asked.

Neil looked uncomfortable.

"I really shouldn't tell you. It's against—"

"I only meant *generally*," Clare insisted. "Just give me an idea."

Neil sipped his pint.

"Actually," he said, "you suggested it to me yourself, last week, at the hospital. You remember I asked you what the word 'blaze' might mean to Angelo?"

"I remember. I said it might be the model of the car that hit him."

"Right. Well, it turns out that there is a car with the model name of 'Blaze' – just one. And luckily, it's quite an obscure car company."

"Would I have heard of it?" Clare asked.

"I doubt it – the car's a Japanese import.

Yakimoto, they're called. Anyway, there are only two of these cars that we know about in the Nottingham area. So we're checking out their owners."

Before Clare could ask anything else, Neil added, "And that's all I can tell you."

"But it looks promising?" Clare pressed him.

"Please," Neil said. "Let's change the subject."

They talked about their old schools and holidays they'd been on – standard first-date stuff. At ten past eleven, Neil drove her home.

"Thank you," she said to him. "I enjoyed myself."

"Can we do it again?" Neil asked, a little nervously.

"Yes. I'd like that."

He leant forward. She thought he was going to give her a peck on the cheek, but then he chickened out. She offered him her hand.

"Good luck with the investigation," she said. "You will let us know if . . ."

"We'll let you know," he said.

All the house lights were still on. Clare went inside to face the usual inquisition. But tonight, it didn't come. Her parents sat alone in front of the TV set, watching the closing credits of *Newsnight* in silence. Dad turned off the set before *The Late Show* began.

"Have they found out anything?" he asked, when Mum had gone upstairs.

Clare shook her head.

"He says they have some promising leads. They're doing their best."

Dad nodded grimly. He kissed Clare on the forehead, then went to bed, walking out of the room slowly, fists clenched inside the pockets of his trousers. Clare put the television back on with the sound low. She watched it until half past one, when her head became bleary and she knew that, finally, she would be able to sleep.

The other workers in Dawn Miller's office confirmed her story. Someone had blocked her in at the car park, and in the process of getting out, she'd scratched her car on a wall.

"She took it very well," the Senior Probation Officer said. "Put a note on the other car's windscreen – 'next time you park behind me, leave a tin-opener so that I can get out'."

This had happened on Wednesday, the day after Angelo's death.

"Didn't look like a wall to me," Neil told Jan. "Maybe she made a song and dance out of it in order to cover herself. Maybe it happened the day before."

"Don't be so cynical," Jan told him. "We'll see this Nick Shears bloke. If he backs up her timings, she's off the hook."

But Nick Shears wasn't home. According to Dawn, he was unemployed.

"Probably working a fiddle somewhere," Jan said.

"Don't be daft," Neil told her. "Just because you're on the dole doesn't mean you've got to stay home all day."

They drove to Sneinton Market, where they were forced to park on a single yellow line outside the Victoria Leisure Centre. Sneinton Market was in full flow. It was only eleven, but some of the punters in the Market Club were already well oiled.

"Brian Boland?" Dave the barman said. "Course I know him. A regular."

"Was he in last Tuesday afternoon?" Neil asked. "I believe you were on."

"He's in every Tuesday afternoon. Does a fair bit of business here then. People know, if they want to find Brian, he'll be around."

"Do you remember what time he left?"

"There you've got me. Sometimes stays till four, five . . . I've known him stay till six."

They talked to three other people who remembered seeing Boland the previous Tuesday. None was certain when he'd left. As the two officers walked out of the club, Jan turned round.

"Oh, by the way," she said to the barman, "where does Brian Boland usually park his car?"

"The car park opposite," Dave told them, in a tone which suggested that the answer was obvious.

"That's the reason he comes on Tuesday afternoons. The market closes early and you can get a parking place."

"So he was lying about the car," Neil said, as they drove back towards Churchfield Lane to see if Nick Shears had returned. "I wonder what else he was lying about?"

"I think," said Jan, "it's time we ran a computer check on Mr Boland."

This time, the door was answered. Nick Shears turned out to be a small, wiry, good-looking guy, with long, curly hair. He didn't look like most drug-dealers Neil dealt with, more like a mechanic, or a plumber.

"Yeah, she came round about ten past four," he told the officers. "Left about three-quarters of an hour later."

"Long visit," Neil said.

"Yeah, well . . . I'd missed a couple. You know how it is."

"Working?" Jan suggested.

Shears laughed.

"Have you tried getting a job round here – with or without a criminal record? There are over four million out of work in this country, if you count all the people the government leave off the books. Did you know that?"

"Yes," said Neil. "I did."

"Thanks for your help," Jan told Shears. "We'll see ourselves out."

"Believe that?" Neil asked as they drove back to the station.

"Why not?" Jan told him. "I can't see many ex-cons wanting to give their probation officer an alibi, unless it were true. Can you?"

Neil shook his head.

"So where does that leave us?"

Jan didn't answer his question. A message was coming through on the radio.

"The suspect you enquired about, Brian Boland, was convicted of driving under the influence of alcohol in May this year. He was fined five hundred pounds and banned from driving for twelve months."

Neil and Jan looked at each other.

"I think we'd better go and see Mr Boland again."

They got to Boland in his office, just as his wife arrived to take him home. Jan confronted him with what they'd found in the National Computer records.

"What you didn't tell us when we spoke last, Mr Boland, was that you'd been banned from driving for twelve months."

"You didn't ask." Boland looked irritatingly smug.

"But your car was outside your office when we

interviewed you, Mr Boland," Neil said. "How do you explain that?"

"My wife drove me to work, then caught the bus herself," Boland replied. "She often does that when the traffic's heavy. You're not very keen on driving, are you, Marjorie?"

"That's right," said Mrs Boland. "I'm not."

Mrs Boland, a primary school teacher, was a hard-faced woman with a matronly figure. Jan could see that they wouldn't get much change from her. But she had to try.

"You have your own car as well, Mrs Boland. Why is that? Why do you keep two cars on?"

"A year's ban doesn't last for ever, Sergeant. Brian's fond of that car. There's not many like it."

"That's true," said Neil, "and that's why, Mr Boland, I'd like to put it to you that, on Tuesday last, your car was involved in a collision at about ten to five in the afternoon, while you were driving, illegally, back from the Market Club."

That was Neil, going in feet first. Jan sighed. She knew what was coming.

"That's impossible," Mrs Boland said before her husband could reply. "Last Tuesday Brian came home on the bus, like he always does from the Market. He'd had a few and went straight to bed to sleep it off. He got home just after I did – half past four."

*   *   *

"Why did you have to mention the time?" Jan asked Neil on their way out. "Now he's got an alibi instead of a faulty memory."

"Oh come on," said Neil. "It's obvious she'll say anything to protect him. You don't really believe he's not driving that car around, do you?"

"Of course not," Jan replied, irritated. "But believing and proving are two different things."

"So where does that leave us?" Neil asked.

"Dawn Miller's in the clear. Boland's our best suspect. We'll give his details to all the foot and car patrols. If anyone sees him driving, he's had it. But as far as the Angelo Coppola case is concerned, we're on shaky ground. He could have done it, but all the evidence is circumstantial and there's the wife's alibi. Also, Boland had no reason to turn onto Bobbers Mill Road."

"A short cut home?"

"For Dawn Miller, yes. But not for Brian Boland. No, I'm afraid that unless something turns up, we've had it."

"Back to square one," Neil suggested.

"Worse than that," Jan told him. "A dead end."

2

Autumn

10

The heat wave broke abruptly, in the second week of September. The children had gone back to school and the streets were suddenly empty. Cold sheets of rain blew across the city. Clare felt trapped inside the house. Dad complained that it was impossible to get work done. Mum sat around, staring into space.

Before long, Clare would be back at university. Yet that life seemed a world away. So much had happened since June. If Angelo were alive, he would be taking his GCSEs this year.

If.

The investigation into Angelo's death was winding down. The "promising leads" which Neil had mentioned seemed to have turned into dust. His sergeant was still responsible for the case – officially – but she had it on a back burner. Clare's patience was wearing thin.

She had been out with Neil twice since their first date. They had some laughs together. Under other circumstances, they might have something more going on than warm conversation and goodnight kisses. But Clare knew it wouldn't last after she went back to university. Neil was keener than she was. Clare meant to let him down gently before time and distance did the job for her. Meanwhile, the house felt like a tomb. The family didn't talk much. The visits of condolence tailed off, and they watched a lot of television. Every time there was any kind of a car chase on the screen, Mum would change the channel.

Clare's going out with Neil made things worse. After each date, when Dad got Clare alone, he would ask her, "Have they got anything? Are they any nearer?"

"No, Dad," she would tell him. "And Neil wouldn't tell me if they were near – not until charges were brought. We have to be patient."

Clare doubted that she was convincing her father of the need to be patient. She certainly wasn't convinced herself. Clare needed to do something, *anything*.

"It's hard to be patient, *tesore*. Not when a hundred things every day remind me of Angelo, and why he isn't here. How can I sleep at night, knowing that my only son is dead and his killer is free? Tell me that."

Clare squeezed his hand.

"But Dad, even if we did find out who did it, we have to leave it to the law. Trying to take our own revenge would only make things worse."

"I'm not talking about revenge," Dad told her. "Revenge is bitter. But I am talking about vengeance, about just retribution. When your Uncle Roberto talked about avenging Angelo's death, I said no – we must leave it to the law. But if the police don't find out who did it . . ."

He put his head into his hands.

"Then what?" Clare asked, softly.

"I don't know," Dad replied.

Clare looked lovelier every time Neil saw her. Tonight, in Browne's wine bar, she wore a black lambswool top with a simple, silver necklace. Neil was sure that every other man in the place envied him.

"A fortnight ago," Clare said to Neil, "you told me you had two promising leads. What happened to them?"

"Their stories checked out," Neil told her. "That's all."

"But you seemed so sure."

Neil grimaced. He had been trying to avoid this

conversation. Jan had warned him – going out with someone who was involved in one of your cases was asking for trouble. But he couldn't help himself.

"Look," he told her. "It's true. There was one person who looked like a very likely candidate, and we're still investigating that person. But, so far, we don't even have circumstantial evidence. No damage to the car, no identification by witnesses, nothing. I don't want to build your hopes up."

"So it's possible," Clare said to him, "that you know who killed my brother, but you can't prove it?"

"No," said Neil. "We can't *know* who killed Angelo without evidence. It's possible that we've *found* your brother's killer, but we have no proof. And without proof, in the eyes of the law, that person is innocent.

"Look," he went on. "I'm afraid that police work is littered with cases where we've got a fairly good idea of who committed a crime, but we can't pin it on them. Now, can we change the subject, please?"

Clare listened while Neil told her a long story about a credit card thief they'd caught in the city. But he could see that her mind was elsewhere. The angry look on her face told him what she was thinking. Telling Clare that they might have already found Angelo's killer, but couldn't prove it, only made things worse.

However, she'd have been angrier still if he'd told her the full story: that Brian Boland was serving a year's suspension of his driving licence for drunken driving. If Boland was the one who knocked over Angelo Coppola, he had probably been over the limit, and driving illegally. In Neil's book, that was cold-blooded murder.

Every traffic cop in Nottingham had been alerted to look out for Boland driving, but, so far, he hadn't been behind a wheel. His wife drove him to work in the morning, in her car, then went on to the school where she worked. Boland's Yakimoto Blaze stayed resolutely parked outside his house.

It was no good knowing that Boland had driven illegally in the past – they had to catch him doing it now. Just a matter of patience, Jan told Neil, but Neil didn't agree. Boland might be an alcoholic, but he wasn't a fool. He would obey the letter of the law until his ban ran out.

It was frustrating, not being able to share all this with Clare. Now, as he asked when he could see her again, Neil sensed hesitancy in Clare's reply.

"Leave it a few days," Clare said. "My friends are feeling neglected. There's only a couple of weeks before we all go back to uni."

"That's what I'm worried about," Neil said, trying not to sound wimpish.

"Don't get too serious," Clare whispered, and kissed him on the cheek.

It was all very well for her to say that, Neil thought, as he watched Clare walk out of the room. If he could hold back his feelings for Clare until he was sure of hers for him, he would. Jan Hunt was always after Neil to think before he acted, and he was getting better, more methodical, in his police work. But falling in love was another matter, out of his control. There was a song he half remembered. How did it go? Something like: *mere reason alone can never explain how the heart behaves*. It was true. He could see that Clare was going to hurt him, but nothing he could do would stop it happening. He was too far gone.

Clare looked through the Yellow Pages section on car dealers. There were thirteen pages, full of ads. Nothing under Yakimoto. This was hardly surprising, she thought. If a dealer had sold only two cars in the last ten years, they'd long since have gone bust. But some dealers handled a variety of different makes. She went through the whole section again, this time with a fine-toothed comb. She found two possible contenders: Glaxon Cars in Arnold, specialists in exclusive imported models; and "Big In Japan", the Japanese car specialists, over in Ilkeston.

Clare took a deep breath, then dialled the first number and asked to speak to the manager.

"Who's calling, please?"

"Clare Coppola. I'm doing a story for BBC Radio news."

At university, Clare did a bit of work for the student radio station.

"How can I help you?" a young, over-confident voice asked.

"Hi. I'm doing a story about what makes people buy obscure cars."

"Then you've come to the right place."

Clare tried to project bubbly enthusiasm.

"Great. I wonder, do you stock a car called the Yakimoto?"

The manager ummed and aahed.

"I'm sure we have done, in the past. Never a big seller. Nothing particularly distinctive about them, you see."

"Would you have a record of the ones you've sold?"

"Our service department would, yes. Why are you interested in that particular make?"

"Er . . . we want to feature cars that nobody's heard of."

The manager started to bore her with details of cars so obscure that she was bound to love them.

"Eastern European cars – they're the coming thing. Not very fast, not very sturdy, but *extremely* environmentally friendly. Now, everyone's heard of the Trabant, but have you heard of—"

"Perhaps it would be a good idea if I came in

to see you," Clare said. "Would this afternoon be all right?"

"Certainly, certainly. Any publicity for our new registration models would be much appreciated."

"And if you could look up the details of the Yakimotos you've sold . . . You see, there's this angle there that I'd like to pursue."

"No problem."

Clare made an appointment, then rang up "Big In Japan". The manager there seemed quite knowledgeable about Yakimotos.

"Nah, don't stock 'em. Thing is, we've only been open three years, and Yakimoto merged with one of the big boys just before then – Toyota, Honda . . . can't remember which. Anyway, they stopped making cars under their own name. No great loss. There was nothing original about their designs. They were a bit cheaper than some of the equivalent models, that's all."

Clare thanked him and hung up. Then she got her bicycle out of the shed in the garden, pumped up the tyres, and put on her cycle clips. As she was wheeling the bike out by the path at the side of the house, Mum called to her: "If you're going out on that, you'd better wear this."

"This" was the cycle helmet that Angelo had been given for his fourteenth birthday. He had worn it for a while, but then complained that he found it too hot during the heat wave. Clare took the helmet, and adjusted the strap so that it fitted her head snugly. At least it'll keep the rain off, she thought.

Cycling to Arnold took her twenty-five minutes. The garage was easy to find. The manager was in his early twenties, with short, straight hair and a baggy designer suit. His tie was almost as loud as his voice.

"BBC not pay well?" the manager asked. "Can't even stand you a taxi?"

"I'm freelance," Clare explained. "I don't get expenses. Anyway, I like cycling."

"To each their own."

Clare had to listen to an endless spiel about the glories of Glaxon Cars and the different makes they serviced and supplied. Dutifully, she took notes in what looked like shorthand, until you tried to read it back. Finally, she asked, "Did you manage to find out about those Yakimotos I mentioned?"

"Sure did, though I don't know why you're so interested. The last one we sold was before my time, just over three years ago. In fact, we've got one in today, having its first MOT. Want a look?"

Clare nodded. What she saw was a small, compact car with bright red metallic paint. She looked all over it for the word "Blaze". It wasn't there.

"Actually, I was particularly interested in another model. The one called Blaze."

"Never heard of it."

Grudgingly, the manager flicked through his card index.

"No, you're right. 'Blaze' is the GTI model – very obscure. We did sell one once. No, I tell a lie. Two."

"Who did you sell them to?"

The manager gave her a funny look.

"Who did you say you were working for again?"

"The BBC. Look, I'll make sure you get some good publicity out of it."

Grudgingly, the manager pulled out the card.

"We'd better. Here they are: the first one brings hers back for regular services. The second one's a cheapskate – never been back since his parts guarantee ran out."

"Thanks," said Clare, hoping that he wouldn't notice how her notes had suddenly become legible. "I appreciate this a lot."

She put her bike helmet back on. The manager handed her his card.

"Aren't you going to give me yours?"

"Haven't got any at the moment. I'm having some more printed up."

He gave Clare a look which said that he wouldn't believe her in a million years.

"How about your phone number, then?"

"Sorry," she told him as she unlocked her bike. "I've got a boyfriend."

Before he could come back on that, she cycled off. She had the information she needed. She was ready to begin.

11

Brian Boland's address turned out to be a smart semi in one of the city's hinterland estates. Parked outside the house was a yellow car. As Clare cycled up to it she saw the lettering, clear as anything, on the wing near the front: Blaze. It really existed. She hadn't expected the car to be there, nor for anyone to be in. She'd only cycled here because it was more or less on her way home.

What to do now? The house looked empty, but she could ring the doorbell, find out. Clare assumed that a man living in a house like this must have a job. But, if so, why had he left his car at home?

She decided to inspect the Yakimoto more closely. There was no sign that it had been in an accident of any kind. She looked inside. Expensive radio-cassette. Leather upholstered seats. Fitted rear seat belts. Nothing out of the ordinary.

Then Clare noticed something, something so obvious that she felt foolish for not spotting it at once. There was some gilt lettering etched onto the rear windscreen, beneath the rear window heater. Clare walked behind the car, trying to look casual, and read what it said: "Boland Associates. Best cover, best prices for all your insurance needs. Call us now on . . ." There was a phone number and an address, on a main road not far from where she was now.

Was Boland the one the police suspected? Clare considered this as she cycled through the spitting rain to Boland's office. The other Yakimoto owner was a woman who lived in Mapperley. Maybe it was her. Clare had expected the driver to be a man, but that was just casual sexism on her part. After all, Boland didn't need to drive down the Alfreton Road to get back from work. Maybe Dawn Miller did.

The office of Boland Associates was above a shop on the Nuthall Road. A metal staircase led up to it. There was a light on inside. All Clare had to do was walk in. But what should she say? If she pretended to be buying insurance, she had no excuse for asking where Boland and his car were one afternoon in August. She would have to make it up as she went along.

Through the office window Clare saw a large man, presumably Boland. He was sitting in a leather-backed swivel chair, talking on the telephone. He waved Clare in.

"Only be a minute," he told her, covering the mouthpiece.

As he talked, Clare was able to get her bearings. It was an ugly, square office which contained little more than three chairs, Boland's desk and a filing cabinet, with a plant pot on top of it. There was a small sink, above which was a calendar showing a semi-clad girl photographed in an exotic location. An electric kettle stood on the drainer, and to the left of that was a small cabinet, presumably containing drink.

"Coffee?" Boland offered, extending his hand once he'd put down the phone. "I saw you looking longingly at the kettle. Horrible weather out there."

"Thanks," Clare said. "I'd appreciate that."

She looked at Boland from behind as he put the kettle on. He was a large, overweight man who slouched. His grey suit was slightly too big for him, and crumpled. He had a bald patch which he'd attempted to comb his brown, greasy hair over.

"Like a drop of something stronger in it to keep out the cold?"

"No, thank you."

"Don't mind if I do?"

Boland opened the drinks cabinet and added half an inch of whisky to his coffee. He gave Clare hers.

"Now, young lady, what can I do for you? No, don't tell me – bicycle insurance?"

Clare smiled graciously and put her cycle helmet on the floor.

"I think it's covered under our household policy, thank you."

Boland nodded.

"Cheapest way. What then?"

Clare put on her most ingratiating voice.

"Actually, I may have taken your coffee under false pretences. I don't want to buy insurance. I'm a freelance reporter, researching a series for the *Evening Post.*"

Boland raised both eyebrows. There was something distinctly slimy about him, Clare thought.

"About insurance?"

"No," Clare told him. "About traffic accidents."

Boland drank half of his coffee down in one gulp.

"I'm not the man you need to see," he told her. "The big boys in town have all the actuarial tables . . ."

"I'm not after statistics," Clare told him. "I'm writing about a specific case – the police gave me your name."

"The police?" Boland looked disturbed.

"Yes. I'm writing about unsolved hit-and-run accidents. I gather that you were one of the people questioned and cleared of involvement in a recent accident of that kind – the Angelo Coppola case."

Boland blinked and nodded.

"Well, it's nice to know that I've been cleared of suspicion," he said. "Nice of the police to tell you that without telling me first. But I'm not sure how I fit into your article, Miss . . . what did you say your name was?"

"Clare," Clare told him. "Clare . . . Foster. The thing is, I'm writing a history of the investigation. Obviously, we hope that it'll jog people's memories and may help the police find the killer . . . that is, driver. But we wouldn't want you to be embarrassed by the publicity. That's why I'm here to get your co-operation."

"I see," said Boland. "OK, then. What do you want to know?"

"Just what you told the police."

Boland lit a cigarette.

"So you haven't seen my statement?"

"Oh no, of course not."

Boland nodded slowly.

"There's not much to tell, really. I was at home when it happened, with my wife. I'd been in the Market Club that afternoon and caught the bus home. End of story."

"Why weren't you in your car?"

"My car?"

"Yes. I believe that the make of your car was what connected you to the investigation."

"Was it now?" Boland seemed disturbed for a moment. "That's interesting. But I don't drive for the time being."

"Why not?"

Boland drained his coffee.

"Too fond of this stuff," he said, pointing at the dregs in his mug. "Got a one-year ban for being over the limit."

Clare tried to conceal her reaction.

"But," Boland added, poking a finger at Clare, "your paper'd better not print that. A driving ban's bad publicity for someone in my trade. People tend to think bad luck's infectious."

"I promise to be discreet," Clare told him, finishing her coffee. "And I won't use up any more of your time. Do I take it that you have no complaints about the way the police handled your involvement in the case?"

"None up till now," Boland said, ambiguously, as he showed her out.

"Thanks for your time," Clare told him.

"You're welcome, Miss Coppola."

Only as Clare was cycling back home did she realize what he'd just called her.

* * *

Neil finished the report and Jan checked it through for him. She corrected a couple of spelling mistakes, but otherwise it was OK.

"So what do I do now?" Neil asked her.

"File it," Jan said. "If anything else comes up, we reopen the case. Otherwise, it stays in the filing cabinet, unsolved."

"What about CID?" Neil asked. "Do we know if they found anything when they were going round the garages?"

"If they'd found anything, they'd have told us," Jan said. "But, just to make sure . . . excuse me, sir."

Neil looked round. Inspector Thompson had come into the room.

"We're just doing the paperwork on the Coppola case, sir. Did CID circulate all the local garages as we requested?"

"Of course they did," the Inspector said, grumpily. "Nothing. Zilch."

"Thank you, sir. Did you want anything?"

"Yes," said Thompson. "I want you in my office, *now!*"

Jan's face paled. She followed the Inspector out. Thompson had a mean temper when you were in the wrong. Neil felt very glad that he wasn't in Jan's shoes.

He filled in form G.126A on the circumstances of the accident. Or, to be more accurate, he filled in those sections he could fill in. A lot of the paperwork assumed that you knew who the driver was. He wrote "0", which meant "not applicable" by the breath test section, then wondered what to do with the next bit, about what kind of driving licence the driver had. He left that section, and the next one, which was headed "Towing and Articulation", and went on to the next bit, which was the shortest. It was headed "Hit and Run".

There were three choices: "0" meant "Not Hit and Run", "1" meant "Driver Aware" and "2" meant "Driver Unaware". Neil wrote a "1" and went on to the next section, "Manoeuvres", where he filled in a "9" for "Turning right". But they didn't know that for sure, so he ticked 18, "Going ahead other", as well. The next few categories were even more difficult. Neil began to chew his pencil, but was interrupted by an angry shout.

"What on earth have you been up to?"

Jan had stormed back into the room, eyes blazing.

"Pardon?" Neil said.

"Tell me something. Have you been talking to a reporter about this case, giving her details about the investigation?"

"No. Of course not."

According to Neil's training, you were allowed to give confidential details of an investigation to the press, as long as they treated it as background, and didn't use it in their story. However, you were advised to avoid doing this, as some reporters couldn't be trusted not to use the information.

"What's happened?" he asked Jan.

"The Inspector's just been taking a complaint from Brian Boland, about his personal life being delved into, all because we gave his name to someone claiming to be an *Evening Post* reporter."

"I haven't . . ."

"Only Boland didn't think she was an *Evening Post* reporter, because he thought he'd seen her on the telly, coming out of the Angelo Coppola inquest."

"Oh no," said Neil. "I swear I didn't—"

"Don't get yourself in any deeper before you hear what she called herself," Jan told him, with a trace of humour in her voice. "The woman claiming to be a reporter said her name was Clare *Foster.*"

Neil sat down and groaned. Part of him felt proud, in an obscure kind of way. The other part felt like he'd just been punched in the stomach.

The car arrived at twenty to six. The house had a garage, but the rain had stopped, and Dawn Miller left the car outside. Perhaps she was planning to go out later. Clare gave the woman two minutes to get inside, then went and looked at the Yakimoto Blaze. There was a blue, circular parking pass on the front, with "Probation Service" written on it. On the front right-hand wing, just in front of the "Blaze" logo, was a scratch, two centimetres thick, twenty centimetres long, slightly crooked. It could have been caused by a collision with a bike.

That was all Clare needed to know for now. She knew what Dawn Miller looked like, and she had seen her car. Presumably Miller was a probation officer, which meant that she knew the law, and would be even less impressed by Clare's claims to be a reporter than Boland was. She had to try a different tack.

When Clare got in, Dad still wasn't home. Mum was in the kitchen. Clare put her bike away then used the phone in the hall. Dawn Miller's number was in the directory. She answered on the second ring.

"Hello?"

"Dawn, this is Sergeant Hunt from the Nottinghamshire Constabulary. We spoke a few days ago."

"Oh, right. Have you had any luck finding your driver yet?"

"I'm afraid not."

"What can I do for you?"

Clare made her voice a bit quavery. Jan Hunt had a quiet, undistinctive voice, with a bit of a Nottingham accent, much like Clare's own.

"This is a bit embarrassing, Dawn, but we're writing up our report and my colleague has mislaid

131

some of the notes from our interview with you. Is it OK if I go over some of the facts with you again?"

"Of course."

"Your movements on the afternoon of the accident."

"I visited a client, Nick Shears, just after four, and left his house just after five, getting home by half past."

"And the address of Nick Shears?"

Dawn told her the address, which was off Churchfield Lane, close to where Angelo had been knocked over. Then she added.

"But you should have it, surely? He told me that you'd interviewed him already."

"Yes, you're right," Clare said. "We do have it somewhere. Have you remembered anything else that might help us with our enquiry?"

"How could I remember anything?" Dawn said. "I didn't see the accident."

"Of course. Well, thanks again for your help."

"No problem."

Dawn Miller hung up. She sounded just a bit defensive, Clare thought. And she was in the vicinity of the accident, at the right time. She must be the one, Clare decided – the one the police thought had done it. All they lacked was the evidence to back up their suspicions. Clare intended to find it. The police might not have any more time to devote to finding her brother's killer, but she did. She wouldn't rest until she'd worked it out.

12

At last Nick Shears came out of his house. It was gone eight and the light was fading, which suited Clare. She followed him at a distance, trying to look as though she knew where she was going. Shears didn't look back. He turned off Churchfield Lane, up Prospect Street. Clare turned the same corner twenty seconds later. Shears was nowhere to be seen. Clare stopped outside the doors of The Pheasant. If Shears hadn't gone into this pub, she'd lost him.

He was there, drinking quietly on his own in a side bar. Nick Shears didn't look like a criminal. He looked more like an actor. He was smaller than average and his brown hair was a little too long for Clare's taste. He had deep, memorable eyes, and a slight, puckered chin. She would guess his age to be about thirty-five.

Clare bought herself a tomato juice and sat near the bar. It would be best if Shears tried to chat her up, rather than the other way round – more natural. She glanced at him, wondering how a girl who wanted to be chatted up in a pub behaved.

She also wondered what crime Nick had committed. Clare was a little hazy about how the probation service worked. As far as she knew, people got put on probation because their crime wasn't serious enough to land them in prison. Maybe Shears was into cheque book fraud, or a similar minor con.

"On the bloody Marys are we, darlin'?"

A burly bloke with a beer gut was grinning at her.

"Want another?"

"No, thank you. I'm waiting for someone."

"Aren't we all?"

The man took the bar stool next to hers. He wasn't going to go away, so Clare stood up and walked across the room.

"Mind if I sit here?"

"Be my guest."

Clare sat down with her back to the bar. She gave Shears her best smile and hoped he would start talking. But he just sat there, staring into his pint.

"Didn't that used to be Players Cigarette factory next to here?" Clare said, finally, looking around in desperation.

"S'right," Shears told her. "This place used to be a lot busier then."

"I'll bet," Clare said.

"I had my first job there," Shears said. "Cutting Gold Leaf. You wouldn't remember those."

Clare shook her head.

"Class cigarette," Shears told her. "They don't make them any more. Came in a bright red packet with a gold trim and a tiny picture of a sailor."

"Is that right?" Clare asked, wondering how long she could affect an interest in obsolete cigarette packets. "And where do you work now?"

"I don't."

"Oh. Sorry."

Shears shrugged.

"Nothing to be sorry about. I get by."

He asked Clare what she did and Clare gave him a spiel about her architecture course, trying all the while to work out how to get the conversation round to the alibi he'd given for Dawn Miller.

"You know," she said, "I've been trying to work out where I've seen you before. At first I thought I'd seen you on TV or something."

"You're kidding."

Clare smiled.

"No, but I think I remember now. I saw you

somewhere with this really good-looking black woman, bit taller than you."

As Clare spoke, she hoped that Shears *had* seen Dawn Miller in public at some time, otherwise this approach was doomed.

"Where would that be?" Shears asked.

He sounded a bit touchy, but then Clare had just brought up the subject of his probation officer.

"Oh, somewhere round here," Clare said. "I live just over the other side of Alfreton Road."

"And why would you remember me and her?"

"Dunno," Clare said. "It just came to me. I guess you must be a memorable couple. She your girl-friend?"

Shears mumbled his eventual reply.

"Not exactly," he said.

"What's her name?" Clare asked, still trying to sound chatty.

"None of your business."

Shears' face turned dark.

"Where are you really from? All that stuff about 'architecture' – don't make me laugh! The DHSS, is it? Or are you a snooper from the probation?"

"No, no. Nothing like . . ."

Clare realized she'd made a mess of it. There was no way now that she'd get him talking about Dawn, or find out what he had told the police.

"I didn't mean to offend you," Clare said, gently. "I'm sorry if . . ."

Shears glared at her. Clare looked at her watch.

"Looks like I've been stood up," she said. "Time for me to go."

Shears said nothing as Clare left. There was something funny going on, she decided. Otherwise, why would he be so touchy about Dawn Miller? He had to be protecting her in some way.

But how? Maybe Dawn Miller had threatened to have Shears sent to prison if he didn't back up her story. One thing she was sure about: she didn't trust Nick Shears. And if she didn't trust him, that meant she didn't trust Dawn Miller's alibi, either.

"Neil called," Mum told Clare when she got in. "He wants to see you."

"He'll have to wait," Clare said. "I told him that I couldn't see him for a few days, that I wanted to spend time with friends."

"And is that where you've just been, seeing friends?"

Clare didn't answer. She didn't want Mum to know about her abortive attempts at an investigation. Mum looked pale and worn these days.

"Listen, Clare," Mum went on. "Neil sounded angry. And I'm concerned about you and him."

"How do you mean?"

Mum folded her arms, the way she did when she was laying down the law.

"This isn't a time for you to be getting serious

with a boy in Nottingham – not with what's just happened. Anyway, you're going back to Manchester soon."

"Who said I was getting serious?"

Mum wouldn't let Clare interrupt.

"But I don't know if Neil knows that. And I don't know if you're only going out with him because you want to find out about the police enquiry into the accident."

Clare acted affronted.

"Where did you get that idea?"

"Something Neil said earlier. I won't let you do it, Clare. Your brother's dead. His death was an accident. Even if they find who caused it, that won't bring Angelo back. We need to get on with our lives."

"But how can we," Clare pleaded, "when whoever knocked Angelo over is still driving around out there? It drives me crazy. It's like I'm obsessed with it. Whatever I'm doing, whatever I'm thinking about, all the time, it just keeps coming at me – someone killed my brother. I can't rest until we find out who it is."

"Don't you understand?" Mum was raising her voice too, now. "I feel the same way. So does your father. But it isn't helping us. All we're doing is building up all this . . . all this impotent rage."

Mum put on her more reasonable voice.

"I know the way some of the family were going

on after the funeral – all that Italian machismo talk about vengeance – but it's just talk, Clare. So, if you're going out with Neil to get closer to the case, I want you to stop. He's a nice boy. He doesn't deserve to be hurt."

"Yes," Clare said. "He is nice."

The truth was that she had become fonder of him than she ever expected to. She went on, "But I'm not in love with him, if that's what you're really asking me."

"Then perhaps it's time you stopped letting him get in any deeper."

"Yes," Clare said. "I mean to. I will."

"When?"

"When I see him. But not tonight. I've got things to think about first."

Before Mum could go on at her again, Clare stomped upstairs to her room. She would stop using Neil to find out about the case, but she wasn't going to forget about finding Angelo's killer. She had to go on. If the police couldn't find the person responsible, she would.

13

Heavy traffic piled along the Nuthall Road as Clare cycled back to Brian Boland's house. She passed the office where he worked and checked to make sure that he was inside. He was.

Two potential hit-and-run drivers: Brian Boland and Dawn Miller. One of them was lying. But which? Clare cycled on to Boland's road. There were no lights on in his house, though it was a gloomy day, so Boland's wife must be at work, wherever that was. Clare could get on with what she had to do.

If someone had told Clare, three weeks ago, that she would be knocking on the doors of total strangers and telling outrageous lies, she would have laughed in their face. But here she was, doing just that. She chose a house further along the road. An old woman opened the door.

"Hello. I'm sorry to bother you."

"What is it?"

The woman held the door open on a chain.

"It's OK. I'm not selling anything. I'm making some enquiries for an insurance company. I only need a minute or two of your time."

The suspicious look didn't fade.

"It's about the man next door but one – a big man, drives a newish yellow car. Do you know him?"

"Only to look at."

This was a relief. Clare had avoided the houses on either side of Boland's in case he was friendly with his neighbours.

'Have you seen him driving his car recently?"

"What do you mean – 'recently'?"

"In the last two or three weeks."

"You say it's about insurance?"

Clare nodded. She hoped that she wouldn't have to explain, because she couldn't.

The old woman smiled.

"I don't like him," she said. "This is a quiet road. He drives up it like he's at a Grand Prix, at all hours. Not this week, though. His wife's been driving him. I've seen her. What is it – he's pretending to be injured or something?"

"I'm not really allowed to explain—"

"He beats her up, you know. I've seen her with a black eye. And she teaches little kiddies—"

"Tell me," Clare interrupted. "When did you last see him driving?"

"It'd be early last week, maybe the weekend."

"And before that, you say he drove all the time?"

"Oh yes, you couldn't miss him."

"Thanks," said Clare. "You've been very helpful, Mrs—"

"Johnson. Are they with you?"

Clare looked round. There, much to her distress, was a police car. Neil Foster was getting out of it.

Clare mumbled something and fled down the path. If she could just slink off, cycle away . . . but Neil had seen her. She had a horrible feeling that he'd come looking for her.

"Get in the car."

"I don't see why—"

"*Get in the car!*"

Clare did as she was told.

"My bike . . ."

"We'll bring you back for it," the woman behind the wheel said. She must be Jan Hunt, Clare realized, Neil's sergeant.

"What do you think you've been playing at?" Neil asked, bitterly.

"I've been finding some things out," Clare said, angrily. "Did you know that, until last week, Brian Boland has been driving his car around quite merrily, despite being banned for drink-driving?"

Jan Hunt stopped the car in front of some garages and turned round to face Clare.

"Yes," she said. "We were aware of that. And we will be dealing with Boland when our investigation into your brother's death is over."

The sergeant put on her official voice.

"You've been obstructing the police in the course of their duties by interfering in this investigation," she told Clare. "Which is an offence. Not only that, but this morning I had a call from a probation officer, wanting to know why one of her clients had been questioned by someone in a pub last night. Mean anything to you?"

Clare was silent. She looked at Neil. He was staring ahead, anger burning in his eyes.

"But that wasn't all Dawn Miller told me," Jan went on.

Clare hung her head.

"She wanted to know if I'd rung her the other evening, because I'd 'lost my notes' about her involvement in the case. How stupid are you, Clare? Presumably you know that it's illegal to impersonate a police officer?"

"It was only a phone call," Clare muttered.

"That makes no difference," Jan said. "Neil, tell her."

Neil turned round, his face red with embarrassment.

"You told Boland that the police had given you details about him. Did I?"

Clare shook her head.

"How did you get them, then?" Jan asked.

"From the garage that sold the car."

"You got me into trouble," Neil said. "I shouldn't have told you anything about the case. People are bound to believe that I told you a lot more than I did."

He raised his voice.

"We're not in some children's TV show, where you can play private detective whenever you fancy it. This is real. What you did might have jeopardized the investigation, as well as mucking up my career."

"I'm sorry," Clare said.

"Sorry isn't enough," Jan told her. "We're going to have to take you to the station so that you can make a statement."

"Whatever you say."

"And after that," Neil told her, "I don't want to see you again. Don't go near Brian Boland, or Dawn Miller, and especially not Nick Shears. Or me, for that matter. Have you got that? We're through."

14

There was a week to go before Clare returned to university. She was looking forward to going back, but felt guilty about feeling that way. Although they didn't talk about it much, it was obvious that Mum and Dad needed her at home. Angelo's death had changed everything.

Dad's work was going through one of its periodic slumps. Normally, things got bad in the winter, but this was September and the only jobs coming in were small ones. Dad was having to lay people off, which he hated to do. Worse, he began to talk about bankruptcy in a fatalistic way Clare hadn't seen before. It was as if Angelo's death had knocked the fight out of him.

Clare was surprised by how much she missed

Neil. It seemed like her relationship with him was the one good thing to have come out of the summer. But he hadn't called her, and she was far too proud to call him. She had kept her promise not to go near Brian Boland or Dawn Miller. There wasn't much choice, since Neil's sergeant had threatened to give her a formal caution for impersonating a police officer if she interfered in the case again. But she hadn't given up.

She went to the newsagents which Angelo used to deliver for. The shop was empty of customers.

"Is there any news?" Mrs Malik asked her. "Have they found anything?"

Clare shook her head.

"It doesn't look like they're going to."

Mrs Malik was sympathetic.

"That's hard on you."

Clare agreed.

"It's hard enough accepting that Angelo's dead. But knowing that the person who did it is just walking round, without being punished at all – it makes me mad. It makes me think that there's no justice. I keep thinking about revenge."

Mrs Malik shook her head.

"My religion teaches me that revenge is bad for the soul. We believe in forgiveness, instead. I know it's hard to do, but—"

Clare couldn't take this.

"What about punishment?"

"Through the courts, yes. But the real punishment is what comes in the next life."

"I'm sorry," Clare told her. "I can't wait that long."

A customer came in.

"Are my photographs ready?" Clare asked.

"Here."

Clare paid for the photographs and put them in her pocket. She chatted with Mrs Malik for a few more minutes about her university course. The Maliks had a daughter a year older than Clare who was studying to be a dentist.

"It's a long time," Mrs Malik said. "But it's worth it in the end, yes?"

"I don't know," Clare said. "I really don't know if anything's worth it any more."

She left the shop and walked down towards Churchfield Lane. She would sit in the churchyard, she thought, look at her photographs and decide on her plan of action.

The road was quiet. Over a month had gone by since the joyriders had accosted her here. Clare guessed that they were back at school now, if they still went. Lost in thought, she crossed the road towards the churchyard.

"Gotcha!"

A rough hand seized Clare's arm and twisted it behind her back.

"Following me again, were you?"

"Stop. You're hurting me."

Nick Shears snarled into her ear.

"I ought to kill you."

"Why?" Clare said, trying to turn and face him. "What have I done?"

"You know full well what you've done, you interfering little—"

He didn't finish, as Clare lifted her knee and managed to catch him in the groin. Shears doubled up in pain and Clare was able to break away from him. She ran as hard as she could.

Back home in her room, after getting her breath back, Clare got out the photographs and looked through them. The camera they'd been taken on was Angelo's. The first pictures she looked at were his. Several were from the day of his fourteeth birthday. Others were shot down at the youth club near his school. Clare recognized a lot of the faces.

Then there were pictures that he'd taken of her, the week she'd come back from university. Angelo kept teasing her about how scruffy she'd become, in her casual student clothes. Clare was struck by how happy she looked in these photos: her on her own, her with Mum, her with Dad, her with Mum and Dad. Then one of Clare standing between Angelo and her father, all of them grinning. It was the last photograph of her brother alive.

Clare put these photographs aside and looked at

the ones she had surreptitiously shot the day before. They were all of a lime green car, and had been taken in the probation office car park. The scratch on the front of the wing had been painted over, but the car was still recognizably Dawn Miller's. Clare stuffed the snaps into her pocket, then took Angelo's photos downstairs to show to her mother.

The way Clare saw it, the police had plenty on Boland. If they could prove that he'd done it, they would. Dawn Miller was another story. As a probation officer, she was practically one of them. Therefore, they wouldn't investigate her seriously. But Clare meant to.

From now on, she was going everywhere on her bicycle. If she came across Nick Shears, she wanted to see him first. Clare had considered telling the police about his threatening behaviour this morning, but couldn't see the point. After all, she had hurt him more than he had hurt her.

Dawn Miller worked the west side of the city. Her clients were in Radford, Basford, Forest Fields and Hyson Green, all areas which were riddled with back-street garages. From what Neil had told Clare at the beginning of the enquiry, the police would have done a routine check on the main garages in the city. But it was unlikely that they'd gone round all the back-street garages, which came and went so quickly.

Back-street garages were the sort of places that would employ people on probation, no questions asked. So Dawn would get to know about them. She'd certainly know enough not to take her damaged car to Glaxon, where she had it serviced. Then, finally, the probation officer could have deliberately scratched her car after having it fixed, because anyone looking at the car would notice the scratch, not the recently repaired bodywork.

"Not been near us," the man at the body shop on Birkin Avenue said. "I'd remember a make like that."

"What did you say was wrong with it? A dented body?" another asked. "Did it want knocking out or a new wing?"

Clare said she didn't know.

"Thing is, a new wing would have to be ordered from Japan."

That would take too long, and it would be on record.

"No," Clare said. "She'd have wanted the bumps knocked out, but so that you couldn't see it had ever been in an accident."

"In that case," the owner told Clare, "you'd want a place that does restoration work, not just resprays and insurance jobs."

He gave her a couple more to try.

*　　*　　*

By evening, Clare had visited a dozen garages, and was exhausted. Her legs wouldn't carry her any further. Her bottom was so sore that she could barely sit down. Tomorrow she would have to go farther afield, but right now she needed a bath.

"Hey, look who it is!"

Clare groaned. She was two minutes from home. A white GTI accelerated past her, then screeched to a halt further down the road, spinning round with its front wheels off the ground, doing a "wheely", a hair-raising turn using the handbrake. Now it was driving towards her. There was no-where for Clare to run. She was as vulnerable as Angelo had been a month ago. Only these boys weren't trying to kill her. More likely, they just wanted to impress her. They were pathetic, Clare thought, trying to blank out her fear. When would they learn?

The car came to a halt centimetres from her front wheel. There were four boys in it. Three of them were Mark Crowston's young cronies. Then there was a fourth, younger one, who she didn't recognize.

"Pity Mark's not here," the driver shouted to Clare. "He was looking forward to seeing you again."

"Leave me alone," Clare told them.

She considered riding on the pavement, but they might still try to get in her way. After all, they weren't bothered about whether they damaged their car.

"Did you find who knocked over your brother yet?" one called out.

Clare didn't reply.

"Dangerous things, bicycles, you know. I'd have thought you'd have learnt that by now."

"Just leave me alone," Clare repeated.

Behind the car, a large van was coming. It hooted for the lads to get out of the way.

"I hope you've taken your cycling proficiency test," another of the boys called out. "Mind you, it didn't help your brother, did it?"

"Why don't you go to hell?" Clare shouted at them, not caring how they responded.

All three boys laughed. Behind them, the van driver put her hand down on the horn. The white car accelerated off. The boys had got the rise they wanted out of Clare. She felt sick. Slowly, she cycled home.

The next day was the first of October, a Friday. Clare could be moving into her flat today if she wanted. Instead, she was cycling around increasingly obscure back streets, visiting increasingly dodgy garages. The people she met were less and less forthcoming. Clare was sure that half of them were involved in breaking up stolen cars for their parts, or respraying them and changing the number plates. The funny thing was, she found her search fascinating. If her cause hadn't been so desperate, she would almost say that she was enjoying herself.

Dad came home for lunch.

"When do you want me to drive you to Manchester?" he asked Clare.

"I'll catch the train on Monday," Clare told him. "There's no need for you to waste your day off."

"Nonsense," Dad told her. "You'll need to take lots of things for your new flat. Anyway, I want to see it."

What he meant was he wanted to make sure that the people she was living with were all girls, like she'd said. Which he wouldn't, because they weren't.

"Really, Dad, I don't have that much stuff. I'd prefer to go on Monday."

"You must be sick of this place by now," Mum said.

"There's something I have to do."

"And what's that?" Mum asked.

Clare didn't answer.

"Haven't you got into enough trouble with the police already?" Mum asked. "You shouldn't be trying to do their job, Clare. You're only hurting yourself, and hurting us, too."

"Maria's right," Clare's father said. "It's time to put it all behind us. Leave it, Clare. Go back to Manchester."

"There's one thing I need to finish," Clare said. "When it's done, I'll feel like I've done everything I could to find . . . to find . . ."

Dad gripped her hand.

"If that's how you feel, do whatever you have to do. But let me drive you to Manchester on Sunday. All right?"

"All right."

There was no point in arguing. Garages wouldn't work on Sunday, anyway. Clare had a day and a half to find the place which had fixed Dawn Miller's car, if it existed.

Neil called round on Saturday morning just as Clare was getting ready to go out. Mum let him in, despite Clare's complaints.

"I look a mess!"

She was wearing the dirty jeans she cycled in and a sweatshirt which was too tight. She was glad to see him, but tried not to show it.

"You look great," Neil told her. He was in uniform.

"More overtime?"

"No. It's my weekend on. I'm driving on my own now."

"Congratulations. Did you come round to tell me that or to remind me that you're still mad at me?"

Neil smiled.

"I've got over being mad at you. I came to say goodbye before you go back to university."

"Goodbye," Clare said.

"Don't be like that. There's something else, too." He looked over at Clare's mum.

"You'd like some coffee, Neil?" Mum asked, tactfully.

"Please."

When she'd gone, Neil leant forward and lowered his voice.

"I thought you'd like to know, Mark Crowston's been sent down. He got a year for the two taking without consent charges we had him on last month, so he'll serve at least six months."

"Good," Clare said, "but that still leaves all the other kids he's taught to steal cars. I saw three of his pals the other day, flashing about in a stolen GTI, trying to give me a scare. How come they got off?"

"They're all younger than him," Neil explained. "And he was the ringleader."

"Well, they've already got a new recruit to replace him," Clare announced, bitterly. "You may have cut off the head but that still leaves a live worm."

"Sometimes," Neil told her, "that's the best you can hope to do. At least we got Crowston."

"But you didn't find out who got my brother."

"No," Neil admitted. "We didn't."

He went on, more tenderly.

"Look, I'm sorry I lost my temper with you last week."

"You had a right to . . ."

Neil acknowledged this with a nervous nod of the head.

"I wondered if I could take you out tonight – finish on a better note."

"I don't think so," Clare said.

"I'd like us to be friends," Neil told her. "I'll be home by half four, if you change your mind."

"I won't."

Neil left just as Mum was bringing in his coffee.

Clare cycled off a few minutes later. This morning, she'd been missing Neil. But now she was annoyed with him. How could he think he could walk back into her life so casually? She would like very much to prove him wrong, to finish the investigation that he'd given up on. But it was no good. She had to admit it to herself – she was on a wild goose chase.

Clare's searches had taken her right to the edge of the city, almost to the Cinderhill roundabout, near to the office where Brian Boland worked. But Boland wouldn't be working on a Saturday. She was unlikely to bump into him. She checked her *A to Z* and wove in and out of back streets. She didn't find any garages. Anyway, even if she did, how would Dawn Miller have known about them? It was time to give up.

Clare checked her map again. She was on one of the countless small private estates that had sprung up all over the city, wherever there was some space. This one wasn't marked on the map. She would have to get out of it by guesswork. She took one street, then another. From the heavy traffic noises, she could guess that she was almost parallel with the Nuthall Road. The next corner would take her to it.

But the next turning was a dead end. Clare was about to turn back when she realized what was in front of her: a block of four workshops, smart ones, with roll-down steel doors, not like the tacky cowboy outfits she'd been visiting for the last few days. Three of them were shut. The fourth was on the verge of closing, as a man in overalls was pulling down the door. Inside the workshop, Clare could see familiar machinery. Above the door, a sign read: *P. Mulhaire*, *Expert Body Repairs*, *Classic Models Restored*.

"Excuse me."

The man, in his twenties, stopped closing the door and looked Clare up and down.

"I don't fix bikes," he said.

"It's not about my bike. Are you Mr Mulhaire?"

"That's right. Paul."

"This won't take a minute. I'm trying to trace whoever repaired a car ..." Clare gave him the vague story she'd invented, claiming that it was a matter of life or death for her brother, who'd been in a collision with the car. She showed him the photographs.

"It's an obscure model," she said. "Would you remember if—"

"Oh, I recognize this one all right," Paul Mulhaire said. "It's a Yakimoto GTI. I did some work on one once, yes. Might have been this one."

"What kind of work?" Clare asked.

Mulhaire shrugged.

"Nothing major. A few dents in the wing, that kind of thing."

"And would you happen to remember who you did it for?"

"I'd have a record, but it's alphabetical – take me a fair while to go through all the names."

"I've got a name you could try," Clare suggested. "Dawn Miller. She's a tall, attractive black woman. Does that ring a bell?"

Mulhaire gave her a grin.

"No. I'd remember her."

Clare was disappointed. But then she thought to ask something else.

"How about Boland, Brian Boland?"

Mulhaire smiled.

"Of course, it's Brian's car. You're right."

"You know him?"

"He puts some insurance work my way. This isn't any kind of trouble for him, is it?"

Clare didn't answer.

"How long ago did you do this work?"

"A month, two months – I'm not sure. During the summer."

"Could you look it up?"

"Can't, I'm afraid. You see, I did it as a favour. I think Brian had had one too many – drove into the back of something when he should have been reversing. Know what I mean?"

Clare was quiet. If she spoke, she would give away her emotions. Mulhaire carried on, chatting like the information he was giving her had no real importance.

"He promised he'd make it up to me by recommending his clients use me . . . Hey, it wasn't you he ran into, was it?"

"No," Clare told him, as the anger welled up inside her. "It was my brother."

15

Neil was taking his uniform off when the phone rang.

"For you!" His mother called. "A girl."

He hurried to the phone.

"Hello?"

"It's me."

Neil's heart lifted.

"I thought you said there was no way you'd be calling me?"

Clare's voice was sombre.

"Something's happened. I've found the proof you need to convict Brian Boland."

Neil groaned.

"I'm not on duty."

"Can't you come round anyway? I'd really rather speak to you. Please."

Exasperated, Neil gave in.

"I'll come. But I hope you aren't clutching at straws, Clare."

"I'm not. Believe me."

Neil hung up, then put his uniform back on, still irritated. Clare was hardly likely to have succeeded where the police force had failed. All the same, he and Jan were sure that Brian Boland was the one who ran over Clare's brother. He would dearly love to be able to prove it.

Clare told her mother the whole story.

"So you think they'll be able to arrest Boland?"

"I don't know," Clare said. "I hope so."

"I'm going to ring Nick," Mum said. "He'll want to be home for this."

Clare went into the front room to wait for Neil. She felt exhilarated. The look of satisfaction on Mum's face when she told her about Boland left Clare feeling – what was the word? – vindicated. People kept saying that the family had to put Angelo's death behind them. Once Boland was behind bars, they could begin to.

The doorbell rang. Clare got up to let Neil in.

The man who barged through the door was not Neil. He was large and ugly and he smelt of whisky. It was Brian Boland.

"I want to talk to you!"

Clare didn't know what to say. Mum came through from the kitchen.

"Who is this?"

Boland's face was red. He began to shout.

"Your daughter's been interfering in my life – lying, pretending to be a reporter, going round my neighbours asking questions about me, then going to my friends, making up stories about me running over her brother."

"They're not made up," Clare snapped.

Boland exploded.

"That's *slander*! I'll have you in court for it!"

"You'll be the first one to appear in court," Clare said quietly.

Boland grabbed Clare's shoulders and began to shake her.

"I want you to leave my life alone, do you hear me!"

"Let go of her!" Mum shouted.

The door opened. Dad stood in the doorway. There was a fierce look on his face which Clare had never seen before.

"Leave my daughter alone," he said.

Boland took a step back.

"Then tell her to leave me alone."

The two men faced up to each other. Boland was a big man, but Dad was bigger.

"Did you kill my son?" Dad asked.

Behind Dad, in the street outside, Clare saw Neil getting out of his car. Boland began to bluster.

"From what the police told me, no one 'killed' your son. He died in an accident, didn't he? Perhaps he'd still be alive if he'd been wearing one of those." Boland was pointing to the cycle helmet which Clare had left on the stairs. Dad's fist was already clenched. Slowly, he raised his arm.

"You . . . you ran him over."

"No."

Before Dad could hit Boland, Neil charged through the open door, between them.

"Stop! What's going on here?"

There were five people crammed into the small hallway now. Clare spoke.

"I found the garage which repaired Brian Boland's car after he ran into Angelo."

"Rubbish," Boland sneered. "That happened weeks before your brother died. I was nowhere near—"

"In that case," Clare interrupted, in a quiet, assured voice, "how come you knew that Angelo wasn't wearing a cycle helmet?"

"I, I must have . . ." Boland ran out of words.

Neil was removing the handcuffs from his pocket.

"Brian Boland," he said, "I'm arresting you for driving a motor vehicle while banned. I will be requiring you to take a breathalyser test, as I suspect you of driving under the influence of alcohol. I am also arresting you for unlawfully causing the death of Angelo Coppola. I must caution you that you do not have to say anything unless you wish to do so, but anything you do say will be taken down and may be given in evidence against you. Do you understand this?"

Boland began to shout obscenities. Neil snapped the handcuffs on.

16

"The papers have to go to the DPP," Neil explained to Clare in the pub that night, "but I'm pretty sure that they'll proceed against Boland. There has to be a better than fifty per cent chance, and a lot of the evidence is circumstantial. Even so . . ."

"How long will he get?"

Neil shrugged.

"If he's found guilty . . . I'm not an expert, but for causing death by reckless driving while banned, even if we can't prove that Boland was over the limit – at least three years. Maybe as many as five."

"It's not a lot for a life, is it?" Clare said.

"It's a lot more than what he would have got if you hadn't traced that garage. You did brilliantly."

Clare tried to be modest about it.

"I didn't think it was Boland, you know. I thought he was too obvious, that if he'd done it, you'd have been bound to catch him. I thought Dawn Miller was the driver, especially after what happened with Nick Shears . . ."

She told Neil about Shears attacking her.

"I couldn't understand why he was so upset," she finished.

Neil smiled.

"I can. Nick Shears and Dawn Miller were having an affair. That's why he was so touchy about the alibi. Dawn hadn't told anyone at the office about her relationship with him. If she had, they wouldn't have let her carry on being his probation officer. Anyway, last week she rang up Jan to tell her. Said she was embarrassed at the time, but now she'd got taken off his case and terminated her relationship with Shears, so she wanted to clear the air. I shouldn't be telling you this, really."

Clare sighed.

"I'm glad you did. No wonder Shears was angry at me. He had every right to be."

"Maybe," Neil said. "But I don't think violence is ever justified, do you?"

"I guess not," Clare said. "Though today, I thought my dad was going to murder Brian Boland. I wouldn't have been upset if he had."

"You would have been when your dad ended up in prison for years and years."

"I guess."

"What now?" Neil asked. "Are you ready to get back to your real life, in Manchester?"

Clare stared out of the window without answering. She made Neil mad sometimes, the way she seemed to be there, but not there. Even on the few occasions that they had kissed, it sometimes felt like she was merely going through the motions. Why did he put up with it? He had humiliated himself, asking her out again only a week after chucking her. His mates said he was behaving like a fool.

But Neil only had to look at Clare to know that she was worth it. Her brother had died, too. That excused a lot. He wouldn't have put up with any other girl treating him in the offhand way she did. But Clare wasn't any other girl. While he had the chance of someone like her, he had to go for it, or he might regret it all his life. Neil decided that he had to ask her now, even though he was sure he already knew the answer.

"What about us?" Neil said, tentatively. "Have we got a future?"

Clare hesitated.

"I don't know," she told him softly.

She gave him an affectionate look. She had treated him more fondly tonight than at any other time in their relationship, but instead of kissing him, she started making speeches.

"Maybe it's best to say that we finish for good. You're all bound up in my mind with what happened to Angelo and I want to put all that behind me. But I really care for you. I want to stay friends, to see you . . . is that an awful thing to ask?"

Neil gave her a rueful smile.

"Not awful," he said. "But difficult."

He leant forward as she leant towards him. Then, gently, they kissed for what he knew would be the last time.

Winter

17

"**D**id you need to bring quite so much stuff with you?" Dad asked, as the car handled heavily on the M1. "You're home for less than a month."

Clare didn't answer. She'd wanted to save her announcement until they got home.

"Cat got your tongue?"

"I'm not going back," she said, in a voice so low it was barely audible.

"Pardon?"

"I said *I'm not going back.*"

That shocked Dad into silence. Quietly, carefully, Clare explained that she'd never really wanted to be an architect, that she'd done it to please him.

"I couldn't keep it up, Dad. Not for all those

years. I'm all grown up now. I have to live for myself."

Dad seemed to be holding back the tears.

"But *tesore*, you can't throw away a *liceo classico*. You could change to another course, one that you'd enjoy more."

"Not this late."

"We'll find the money. Nothing's too good for—"

Clare stopped him.

"Dad, I don't want to be a student. Not that kind, anyway . . ."

"But what are you going to do?" Dad pleaded. "There are millions and millions of people unemployed."

It was too early to tell him. Mum needed to be there, too.

"Then I'll be one of them for a while, Dad. There's no shame in that."

"I won't allow it. I'll find you a job with the family. Angelo's always needing a secretary in Bedford. We'll find—"

"I didn't get all those 'A' levels just to be a secretary, Dad."

"Then what?"

"Watch the road, Dad. It's busy."

It was a cold December day. Every so often fog descended, but the cars around Dad's estate hardly slowed down. Even fewer put their fog lights on.

It was scary. Clare tuned the radio to a local station for the traffic reports. They drove the rest of the journey in silence.

Mum hugged Clare when she got out of the car. Nevertheless, she seemed gloomy.

"What is it, Mum?"

Mum took a brown envelope from the hall table.

"This came by the second post."

The letter informed the Coppolas that Brian Boland would be tried at the end of February.

"How can it take so long?" Dad asked. "Every time people talk to me, especially the family, they ask 'has it come to trial yet? How long did he get?' And I can't answer. I want it behind us."

"We all do," Clare said. "But Boland's in gaol. There's always a backlog of cases. At least now we know when the trial is."

"Clare's right," Mum said. "Only two more months."

They sat down and drank coffee.

"Clare's got something to tell you," Dad announced.

Mum gave Clare a searching look.

"What is it?"

"I'm not going back to university."

"Over my dead body you're not," Mum snapped back.

"It's too late, Mum," Clare insisted. "I've already packed it in."

Mum looked even angrier.

"Why?"

"I couldn't get involved in the course. I realized that I didn't want to be an architect. I want to do something more useful with my life."

Mum put her hands on Clare's shoulders.

"I knew something was up from the way you clammed up whenever I asked you about your studies on the phone. But don't throw it all away, Clare. Do you know what I'd have given to have the chances that you've got?"

"I know."

Mum began to speak more urgently.

"Has it occurred to you that the way you're feeling at university might be bound up with Angelo's death? They call it delayed shock. It's a common thing, a kind of depression. But you'll come out of it, Clare. Don't make a hasty decision that could ruin your life. There are other courses. Take a year off. Think about it. Nick?"

Dad nodded.

"Your mother's right, Clare. It's a lot to give up. Have you even thought about what you're going to do instead?"

"I have," Clare said. "I've already applied and had an interview. I'm waiting for the results of the exam."

"What exam?"

"They tried to persuade me to finish my degree

first, said it would stand me in good stead. But I told them I'd had enough of academia."

Both Mum and Dad looked bemused.

"What are you going on about?" Mum asked.

Clare smiled.

"I'll be staying in the county," she told them, proudly. "I'm going to be a policewoman."

18

The court house was a recent building on the edge of the city centre, between the bus and train stations. You had to cross a five-lane road to get to it. From outside the place looked like a small office block, but inside it was airy and spacious. A guard searched Clare's bag, then ran a metal detector up and down her body – as though, she thought, she were likely to bring in a gun and shoot Boland if the verdict went the wrong way.

In films, court houses were always hectic, crowded places, but this one was incredibly quiet. The decor was calming – all polished wood surrounded by cream and grey, with muted blue carpets. Six out of the nine crown courts were not in use. Clare joined her mum and dad outside

Court Six. Around a corner, she could see Neil, awkwardly waiting to begin his evidence.

It was five past two. People began to go in for the afternoon session. It was the third day of the trial. Apart from the Coppolas and a solitary reporter, there were no regular onlookers. Today, however, there was a teacher with five school kids. The usher checked that none of the visitors were witnesses, then made sure that the kids were all over fourteen.

The school party sat by the door, facing the far wall and the judge's red chair. Clare and her parents were directed to a long row, behind the press seats, facing the barristers and solicitors in the middle of the small, square courtroom. Beyond the lawyers were the twelve seats reserved for the jury.

Everyone rose as the judge came in for the afternoon session. Then the jury took their places. Clare couldn't help but keep looking at them as the trial went on. Seven men, five women. Half of them looked like they were concentrating on every point. Clare wasn't so sure about the rest.

The atmosphere in the court was unreal to Clare, like watching a play on television. She couldn't tell how the trial was going. Earlier, a doctor had given evidence. So had Jan Hunt, Boland's wife, and several witnesses to the accident. Still to come were Neil, the mechanic and (presuming that he took the stand) Boland himself.

It still made Neil nervous when he had to give evidence. He'd be glad when it was all over, especially with Clare watching him, only a few metres away. Boland had hired a good brief. After lunch, in the conference room outside, the Counsel for the Prosecution had warned Neil that they would try to take him apart.

"Just stick to the facts, officer, and you won't go wrong."

But now Neil was in the witness box, under cross-examination, and the facts seemed slippery, two-faced things.

"You did not see my client's car, did you, Constable, on the afternoon of the accident?"

"I couldn't have seen the car because—"

"A simple 'yes' or 'no' will suffice, thank you, Constable."

"No."

"And none of the witnesses identified either my client or his car, is that correct?"

"Yes."

"Indeed, you have been unable to establish any reason why Brian Boland should have driven on Bobbers Mill Road on the day in question?"

"That's true, but—"

"So your only way of connecting my client to this unfortunate accident was an ambiguous bit of hearsay from the deceased?"

"I wouldn't say it was ambiguous."

"No?" The barrister's tone was withering. "You knew this young man well, did you? Well enough to be sure exactly what he meant to say when he was injured, indeed fatally brain damaged and on the verge of losing consciousness for the last time?"

Neil didn't reply.

"In fact, you'd never seen him before, had you?"

"No."

"The word that you say he used – 'blaze' – did you check whether it might have any connotations other than as the name of a model of car?"

"Pardon?"

Neil wasn't sure what the word "connotation" meant.

"You assumed that 'blaze' referred to the car."

"It seemed a reasonable assumption, yes."

"It didn't occur to you, Constable, that, Angelo Coppola being of Italian descent, the word might have, unbeknownst to you, a separate meaning in Italian?"

Neil didn't answer. He hated the way the barrister kept stressing his rank, as though to show how junior the prosecution's chief witness was.

"Very well. Let us move on to some of your other dubious conjectures."

As the barrister leafed through his papers, Neil remembered that he *had* questioned the Coppolas about whether the word "blaze" had any special meaning to them, as soon as they'd arrived in the hospital. But it was too late to bring it up now.

"You say that my client observed that Angelo Coppola might not have died had he been wearing a bicycle helmet?"

"Yes."

"And this was one of your principal reasons for arresting him?"

"Along with the evidence about the repairs done to his car, yes."

"I see. You told Mr Boland that the information about the helmet had not been reported?"

"Yes."

"Then perhaps, Constable, you'd like to explain this video, which, with the court's permission, we will call exhibit three."

A large-screen TV and video was wheeled in. Neil had no idea what the video would be.

Central News flashed onto the screen. It was a report on the Angelo Coppola inquest. A reporter was speaking to camera.

"It emerged during the inquest that Angelo Coppola was not wearing a cycle helmet, which might have saved his life – a clear message there for all paper-boys and girls in the country."

The picture cut to where Nick Coppola condemned the coroner's verdict and pleaded for information that would lead to the arrest of his son's killer. Clare was standing in the background.

In a box at the back of the court, Boland smiled. The tape was switched off.

"Well, Constable. . . ?"

Neil became angry.

"I haven't seen that report before," he snapped. Then he added, brusquely, "The reporter was wrong, anyway. Helmets only protect against cuts and fractures – they're no protection against the severe shaking up the brain gets in a high-speed impact like the one that killed Angelo Coppola."

The barrister smiled.

"Thank you for that expert testimony, Constable. However, you must accept that my client, who watched this broadcast along with several hundred thousand other viewers, demonstrated no special knowledge of the case."

Neil was silent. The barrister smiled smugly.

"I'll take that for a 'yes'. One last point, Constable Foster. Although you had no knowledge of the Coppolas before the accident, is it not true that shortly afterwards Clare Coppola – the deceased's sister – became your girlfriend?"

Neil felt himself blushing, but there was nothing he could do to stop himself.

"For a while, yes."

"So you had a particular incentive to find the driver of the car, did you not?"

"It made no difference to—"

"In fact, it was Clare Coppola who found the so-called evidence about the repairs to my client's car. Is that correct?"

"Yes."

"Would you say that your judgement when it comes to matters pertaining to Clare Coppola was entirely, er . . . disinterested?"

"I would say that I acted within the guidelines at all times."

Again, that horrible smug smile.

"Oh come, come, Constable. You've just admitted that one of your main reasons for arresting my client was bogus. Is it not also the case that, during the case, you were given a verbal warning for revealing confidential information about the investigation to the victim's sister – your girlfriend?"

"Well, er . . ."

"And that Clare Coppola, your then girlfriend, impersonated a reporter in order to get Mr Boland to reveal information about the case?"

Before Neil could reply, the prosecution counsel at last stood up.

"I object. I don't see what relevance such tittle-tattle has."

Before the judge could rule, the defence barrister gave a majestic shrug.

"I withdraw the question. I have no further questions for this witness."

"You may step down," Neil was told.

Neil walked out of the court, avoiding Clare's gaze. He didn't need her to tell him that he'd made a pig's ear of the whole thing.

They didn't talk about the court case much on the way home. However, in the evening, Dad began to talk about a story he'd heard on the radio. A lorry driver ran over a twelve-year-old boy on his bicycle. He'd actually seen what he was doing and, rather than stop in time, risking capture, he drove on, crushing the boy to death. At the trial it emerged that the man had never even held a driving licence. He only got eighteen months. To make matters worse, when the driver got out, he went on driving a lorry, illegally, and gave a V-sign whenever he saw his victim's father.

"Anyway," Dad said, "one morning the father wakes up to find that someone's left a loaded shotgun on his doorstep. He knows what it's about. Someone with a grudge against the lorry driver left it there. But something snaps inside the father. He picks up the shotgun, gets in his car, and goes to where the driver lives. He waits in his car till he sees him."

"And what happened then?" Clare asked. "Did he kill him?"

Dad shook his head.

"Finally the father sees the driver walking down the street with his girlfriend. He gets out of the car with the gun. But the driver sees him. He grabs his girlfriend and covers himself with her. Can you imagine a more cowardly act? In Italy, any man who could do a thing like that . . . there isn't a word low enough. Eventually, the man lets his girlfriend go, and makes a run for it. The father shoots."

"Did he die?" Clare asked.

Dad shook his head.

"He was badly hurt, but he lived."

"And what about the father?" Mum asked, in a bitter voice. "What happened to him?"

"He was tried for attempted murder," Dad told her, "and grievous bodily harm. He pleaded innocent to both charges."

"But how could he do that?" Clare asked. "After all, he did it."

Dad shook his head slowly.

"I don't know. Maybe he claimed that the balance of his mind was momentarily disturbed, although – obviously – he had planned the shooting, waited in the car, and so on."

"What sentence did he get?" Mum asked.

"No sentence," Dad replied with a smile. "The jury found him 'not guilty' on both counts."

Mum nodded.

"I remember the case now," she said. "It's odd how things don't sink in at the time, but later they come to mean so much more to you."

Clare agreed.

"But Boland won't get off with eighteen months, will he? I mean . . ."

Dad shrugged again.

"They've got the breathalyser results from when he came round to our house, as well as all the witnesses to his driving while banned. That has to be worth a prison sentence. But when it comes to running over Angelo . . ."

"He did it," Mum said, firmly.

"I know he did it," Dad said. "And so does anybody who's been following the case. But they have to prove it, beyond a reasonable doubt, and after . . ."

He didn't say "after Neil's evidence today". He didn't need to, Clare thought. But the trial wasn't over yet.

"Your full name, please."

"Paul Mulhaire."

"And your occupation."

"Mechanic."

"This summer you repaired a car for someone in this courtroom. Can you point that person out?"

Mulhaire pointed to Brian Boland.

"Could you tell us the nature of the repairs, please, Mr Mulhaire?"

"Ah, it was just knocking out a few dents on one of the wings."

"Which wing?"

"I don't rightly remember."

Clare noted the way that Mulhaire was exaggerating his Irish accent. This wasn't the way he'd spoken to her at the garage. He was trying to make himself sound stupid. And he'd been certain about which wing it was when he'd spoken to her.

"And these repairs, were they to the front of the wing?"

"Ah, no. I'd say they were more to the side."

"What kind of dents were they?"

Mulhaire scratched his chin.

"I'd say they were more like scratches – like he'd scraped a wall, something like that."

The prosecution counsel was frowning now. Clearly, he was thinking the same thing as Clare – Boland had got to Mulhaire.

"In your statement, you said that you did this job for Mr Boland in late summer."

"I said that, yes. Though, now I think of it, the job may have been as far back as June."

"And it didn't go through your books, did it? That's why there's no record."

"That's right. It was a favour."

"In fact, isn't it the case that the accused put pressure on you to do the work without keeping any record of it?"

"I suppose."

"As though he had a secret to keep?"

Mulhaire smiled.

"Hell, no. I knew he'd been banned from driving – that was why he couldn't do it on the insurance. All he was bothered about was not having to spend his own money!"

The jury laughed. Clare's heart sank.

19

To Clare's surprise, Boland didn't take the witness stand. The following morning, closing arguments were made, the judge summed up, and the jury were sent out. The three Coppolas sat in the grey upholstered seats outside the courtroom, waiting for the twelve men and women to return. They were still out at ten past two, when Neil showed up. He'd just come off duty and was in uniform. Clare told him what had happened.

"I wasn't much good yesterday," he said. "I'm sorry."

"You've no reason to be sorry," she told him. "The things you got caught out on weren't your fault. If anything, they were mine."

He squeezed her hand.

"Whatever happens," he said, "it'll be all over once the jury come back."

Clare stared at the floor as she mumbled her reply.

"Will it?"

The jury returned after deliberating for two hours. Clare could read nothing into their expressions. They didn't look at Boland as he was brought back in. But they didn't look away from him, either.

Boland had already pleaded guilty to driving under the influence of alcohol and driving while being banned. There was only one thing for the jury to decide.

"On the charge of causing death by reckless driving, how do you find?"

The forewoman spoke clearly.

"We find the defendant 'not guilty'."

As the judge thanked the jury, Mum began to cry. Clare put her arm around her. She felt numb. The jury, she noticed, were all studiously avoiding looking towards them. On the other side of Mum, Dad stood up.

"This man murdered my son!" he shouted at the jury. "How can you let him go free?"

"Sit down, please," the judge told him. "I don't want to have you taken out."

Dad sat, as tears started streaming down his face. The judge turned to Boland.

"Mr Boland, do you have anything to say before I pass sentence?"

Boland shook his head slowly. The judge took a deep breath, then spoke.

"Brian Boland, you have been found guilty of driving while disqualified, and driving while under the influence of alcohol, the crime for which you were first disqualified. Although you have been found not guilty of the larger crime, causing death by reckless driving, it is undoubtedly the case that you put the lives of others at risk.

"You chose not to give evidence yourself. The jury were not allowed to read anything into this, but I am. You have had the opportunity to show some remorse for your actions, and have not taken it. You need to be warned, in the strongest terms, not to offend again.

"You will be disqualified from driving for a further three years when your current ban runs out. In addition to this, you will serve a prison sentence of nine months."

Boland's face showed no emotion.

"Nine months," Clare said to Neil as they made their way out of the court house. "That's something."

"Not really," Neil told her, apologetically. "Most people get out between half and two-thirds of the way through their sentences. Boland's been inside on remand for nearly five months. He'll be out within a week. A month at the most."

20

Clare was already waiting for Neil when he got to The Peacock. Three days had gone by since the trial and she looked happier, more alive. For a few moments, Neil felt optimistic. He'd given up on her, but sometimes the moment you gave up was precisely the moment you found what you were looking for.

"I've got something to tell you," Clare said. "It's why I agreed to meet you, really."

"I've got something to tell you, too," Neil said. "But it's not good news."

The barman arrived with their drinks, which Clare insisted on paying for.

"Shouldn't you have gone back to university?" Neil asked.

Clare shook her head.

"That was what I wanted to tell you about. I'm not going back."

"No?"

Neil's first thought was: she's met someone – she's getting married and she wants to let me down lightly before I hear it from someone else. Then she told him.

"I start at Ryton next month."

"Ryton?"

Clare nodded. Neil was incredulous.

"You're joining the police?"

Clare smiled.

"I had my second interview last week. I wanted you to hear it from me first."

Neil shook his head in disbelief. As he tried to picture Clare as a WPC he said the first words which came into his head.

"You'll look terrible in a uniform. They'll make you cut your hair. It won't suit you at all."

Clare gave him a half-quizzical, half-annoyed look.

"That's part of the reason I couldn't keep going out with you, Neil. You're more concerned about the way I look than what's in my mind. Do you really think that the uniform had anything to do with my decision?"

"No," he said. "I don't. But what did make you decide to join up? The last six months haven't exactly been a great advertisement for the police force, have they?"

Clare shook her head.

"But I did realize that I wanted to do something useful with my life. As an architect, I might earn a lot of money. I might get to design homes or churches – things I could be proud of. But I'm more likely to find myself drawing up office blocks and supermarkets, or extensions to people's homes. In the police force you make a real difference to people's lives."

"Do we?" Neil asked, bitterly. "Most of them seem to hate us. You go into court these days, and a jury's going to believe that you've made half your evidence up, because that's what they've seen on TV. And it's worse for women – the villains are less scared of them, so they're more likely to have a go at you."

Clare thought he'd finished, but, as it turned out, he'd only just started.

"Half the PCs will call you a 'plonk' or a 'relief bicycle'. They'll give you all kinds of grief, and you'll have to take it or be treated like a leper. The other half'll hate you for being around because it makes them feel more vulnerable. And women have real trouble getting promoted. Not surprising, since most of them leave after five years or so.

"Did I tell you about my sarge, Jan? She's off on

195

maternity leave. It's only six months since she got promoted. She'll not be back, I'll bet. I'm not trying to put you off, Clare, but—"

"Aren't you?" Clare laughed. "Sounds like it to me, but you're too late. I've signed up, and it's partly your fault – you're the one who made the job sound really good in the first place."

Only because I was trying to impress you, Neil thought, but he didn't say this. He changed the subject.

"How are your parents taking the result of the trial?" he asked.

Clare's confident mood evaporated.

"Mum's been really depressed. She hardly says anything. The doctor's prescribed tranquillizers but I don't think she's been taking them. Friends call round and she won't talk to them. Dad does his best, but he's had to go back to work. The firm's in a rough state at the moment."

"And how's he taking it himself?"

Clare turned the corners of her mouth down.

"Better than I expected. But he keeps getting calls from people in the community, which don't help. They've heard about it through the paper or on the news, and you can imagine what they're like – goading him to do some damage to Boland, or offering to do it themselves. 'A matter of honour' – that's what they say. They've seen too many 'Godfather' movies. As though hurting that slime could avenge Angelo! All it would do is put my dad in prison."

Neil was concerned.

"Do you think he'll do anything rash?"

"I don't," Clare said. "I mean, Boland had a fair trial, and Dad respects that. He keeps repeating: *Vengeance is mine; I will repay, saith the Lord.* Boland *was* found 'not guilty'. I guess that means there was a reasonable doubt about whether he did it or not. I mean, maybe – just maybe – he *is* innocent."

"But you don't really believe that, do you?" Neil asked.

"No," Clare replied. "I don't."

Neil was lost for conversation. He supposed that he ought to congratulate Clare on joining the force. She'd make a good officer, he thought. With her education, she was bound to do better than him, despite being a woman. But he would rather that she wasn't always going to be around, working on the same patch as him. If he was going to get over her, it wouldn't be any easier when there was always a chance of them running into each other at work.

"Anyway," said Clare, more cheerfully, "what was your news?"

"I'm afraid it's about Boland," Neil told her, in his most sober voice. "They're releasing him from prison tomorrow."

21

Clare woke late on Saturday. The night before, when she'd told Mum and Dad about Boland's release, had been an awful one. Dad demolished a litre bottle of *chianti classico* on his own. He kept cursing in Italian. Mum closed up on herself and refused to speak. Clare was stuck in the middle, unable to help and increasingly angry.

She looked at her watch. Ten. Downstairs, Mum was sitting behind the kitchen table, pasty faced. She was wearing her best cashmere sweater with a scruffy apron over it. Everything in the kitchen was spotless. It looked as though she'd been cleaning since dawn. Clare went over and put her arm around her.

"Are you OK, Mum?"

Mum gave Clare a weak smile.

"I'm all right now. It'll take me a while to get over things. But I'm OK."

"Did Dad go off to work?"

"Yes. An hour ago."

"I'll bet he had a bad head."

Clare smiled. Mum didn't smile back.

"Yes. He did have a headache, now that you mention it."

It was as though Mum had forgotten the previous night. Clare put the kettle on.

"I think I'll make myself a coffee and take it back to bed with the paper."

Mum stood up as though Clare had given her an urgent mission.

"I'll make you some proper coffee. It'll only take a second."

"No, really," Clare said. "Instant is fine. Do you want some?"

Mum shook her head.

"Why don't you go back to bed, Mum? You look shattered."

"I'm fine. Just a little tired."

As Clare poured boiling water onto coffee granules, Mum asked:

"Will he be out now, do you think?"

"Boland? I expect so," Clare told her. "I think they release them early in the morning."

"And will there be lots of reporters there, like at the inquest?"

"I doubt it," Clare said. "He's not big enough news."

"He ought to be," Mum said.

"Yes," Clare agreed. "He ought to be."

There was nothing in the paper that interested Clare. A time would come, she thought, when world events would seem relevant to her again. But not yet. Downstairs, she heard electrical noises. Mum must have found some kitchen jobs that she hadn't already done. Clare supposed that it was good therapy. Then the noises stopped.

A minute later, Clare heard the front door slam. She sat up. Mum hadn't left the house since the trial. Something was wrong. Hurriedly, she pulled some clothes on and rushed downstairs. I'm being silly, she tried to tell herself. Mum's just gone out for milk or sugar.

The first thing she saw was the electric knife sharpener, still plugged in on the kitchen table. She looked over to the block next to the sink. One knife was missing – the biggest one.

"God, no!" she said aloud. "No, no, no, no, no!"

Clare wasn't conscious of deciding what to do, but she acted with great speed. She pulled on her coat, took the spare key off the hook and went out into the back yard. There was no time for a cycle helmet, no time for gloves. She pushed the bike out through the narrow back passageway onto the street. She had no cycle clips, so she tucked her jeans into her socks, then mounted her bike.

At least Mum couldn't drive. That was something. She would have to catch a bus, or hail a taxi on Alfreton Road. Clare hoped it was the bus. On a good day, on a bicycle, you could overtake a bus, because it had to keep stopping.

She got to the bottom of the road. There was no one waiting at the bus stop, which meant that one had probably just gone. The traffic lights were changing. She cycled quickly across as cars began to thunder towards her.

Clare cycled as fast as she could, away from the junction where Angelo had been knocked down. After all her searches for garages, she knew this area like the back of her hand. There was a short cut across the Whitemoor Estate, where Mark Crowston lived, which would save her a little time. She could get to Boland's house before Mum did – if Mum was in a bus, not a taxi. Taking deep breaths, Clare cycled even faster.

Without gloves, her hands were cold. Soon her fingers were so numb that it was hard to change gears, but she kept going. She kept thinking about what Mum had in mind to do. Part of Clare badly wanted Mum to get there before she did, she wanted to wound, or even kill, Boland. After all, he deserved it. And any jury in the country would see that Mum wasn't in her right mind. They'd let her off. Wouldn't they?

At the corner of Western Boulevard was a big, complicated junction which was just too dangerous to navigate on a bike. Reluctantly, Clare got off, waited, and crossed at two sets of pedestrian lights. Then she cycled like crazy down a footpath into the Whitemoor Estate.

Here, the roads were quiet, almost empty. There had been a frost in the night and most of the cars were iced up, going nowhere. Clare nearly skidded a couple of times, as she hurtled towards the other side of the estate. She was going so fast that she nearly didn't notice the car which shot out of a side road, far too quickly. It parked a little way in front of her, honking its horn.

Clare recognized two of the lads who got out of this car, an old Ford Escort. They were the friends of Crowston who'd harassed her when she was out cycling in September. Normally, she would have taken a detour, anything to avoid them. But today they were in her way.

As it turned out, the youths didn't seem to notice Clare. The joyriders were preoccupied by a thin boy, with a tousle of red hair, who had opened the door to them. Clare thought she recognized him. He had been round to the Coppola house once or twice, a friend of Angelo's: Steven . . . she couldn't remember his surname, but something made her slow down as she passed his house. She heard a snatch of the lads' conversation from the doorway.

"I'm not coming out."

"Come on. It's Saturday. We'll have a laugh."

"I told you, I'm not coming out."

Then she was out of earshot. Before accelerating again, Clare glanced behind her. The boy who had remained in the car was leaning out of the passenger window. He yelled:

"Don't be a coward. Come out for a run, Blaze!"

"I told you never to call me that!" the red-haired boy snapped back.

A deathly cold ran down Clare's spine. She looked back, then cycled, cycled even faster, cycled faster than she'd known it was possible to cycle. She had to prevent her mother from committing murder.

22

The yellow Yakimoto Blaze which hadn't run over Clare's brother stood in front of the Boland house. There was no sign of Mum. For a moment it seemed to Clare that the whole thing was a dream. If this car hadn't killed Angelo, then Angelo couldn't be dead. How could he have been run over by one of his own schoolmates?

Clare dropped her bike on the pavement outside the house and ran up the path. She pounded on the front door.

"Hold on!"

A woman's voice.

"Hurry!" Clare shouted.

Mrs Boland answered the door.

"Yes?"

"Is your husband back?"

Mrs Boland gave Clare an angry, impatient look. "Back? Yes, like I told the woman who just came. He's gone to his office, and that's where you should go if you've got any business with him."

"You say 'just came'," Clare said, urgently. "How long ago?"

"Five, ten minutes . . . hold on, I saw you in court, didn't I? Aren't you . . ."

"Call the police," Clare said, firmly. "Tell them that your husband's life is in danger. I'm sorry, I haven't time to explain. But do it *now*, please."

Before Mrs Boland could respond Clare was down the path, clambering onto her bicycle.

Boland's office was only five minutes' cycle ride away at the most. Clare should be able to beat Mum there, unless Mum was running. Clare had never known her mother to run anywhere in her life. But this morning, if Mum could sharpen a knife and take it out to harm someone, then anything was possible.

Clare turned onto another road. Still no sign of Mum. She was almost at Nuthall Road now. Maybe the police had got to her already. But they wouldn't have done. Even in the most urgent cases, average response time was five minutes, unless a police car happened to be in the right place at the right time.

There was ice on the road and a vehicle was

approaching from a side road. Its side windows hadn't had the ice scraped off, Clare saw. The driver didn't notice her. He kept driving, straight in front of her, as though she wasn't there. Clare braked sharply, but she was going too fast, and skidded. Her bike hit the car side on.

"Silly cow! What do you think you're playing at?"

Clare picked herself up off the ground. Her head ached. There was a muddy stain all the way down her jeans which she knew would translate into a black bruise on her leg. She was too shocked to be angry.

The driver got out.

"Look! You've scratched my car!"

Clare got up. Her bike was lying in the middle of the road. The frame had buckled. It was useless.

"You drove straight into me," she said to the man. "It was your fault. You've destroyed my bike."

The driver sneered.

"You know where you can go," he told her, getting back into the car.

"Wait!"

The man made an obscene gesture and drove off, at speed. He hadn't even asked if she was all right. Clare picked up her bike and moved it to the side of the road, irrationally blaming herself. If she'd been wearing a helmet, her head wouldn't hurt so much. Angrily, she realized that she hadn't taken note of the car's registration number. Then she remembered why she'd been in such a hurry in the first place.

Nuthall Road was less than a hundred metres away, but every step cost Clare a gnawing pain in her leg and side. Even so, she ran or, rather, stumbled, a short pace at a time. She knew that she was almost certainly going to be too late, but continued all the same. By the time she reached the corner of the main road, the whole right side of her body was in agony.

A police car was coming down Nuthall Road, its siren bellowing. Clare looked up to Boland's office. There, at that very moment, was her mother, at the top of the steps leading to the insurance agent's door.

"Mum!" Clare screamed. "No!"

But the traffic noise was too high. She continued shouting as she forced her body to take her to the steps.

The police car pulled up alongside Clare. She was at the foot of the steps now. There was a railing, which she could use to pull herself up the staircase. Maybe, if she was lucky, there was still time.

"Clare?"

It was Neil. Of course it would be Neil.

"It's my mum," Clare panted, as she yanked herself up another step. "I've got to stop her."

"Let me by. I'll help her."

Neil was behind her now. There was another officer with him.

"No," Clare insisted. "It's not her who needs helping."

Clare could see over the top of the stairs. As she pulled herself up the last two steps she saw Boland, behind his desk, recognition slowly spreading across his face. Next, he looked beyond Mum. He must have seen Clare, with two police officers standing behind her. His face betrayed confusion, nothing more. Then he turned back to Clare's mother. That was when he saw the knife coming towards him. Sat in his chair, legs beneath the desk, Boland was temporarily trapped, unable to move out of the way quickly enough. His face turned white.

"Mum, no!"

Clare was through the door as Mum raised the knife. She was too far away for Clare to grab her.

"It wasn't him, Mum! He didn't kill Angelo. It wasn't him, I swear. It was someone else!"

The hesitation was enough for Brian Boland to pull his chair back and get out of the way. The two police officers ran into the room, between Boland and Maria Coppola.

"Drop the knife, Mum."

"Are you sure?" Mum asked, in a hollow voice.

"I'm sure. Someone else did it. I've found out who it was."

Clare's mother did as her daughter asked. Clare picked the knife up and handed it to Neil. Then she hugged her mother, who was crying.

"I'm sorry," Mum was saying. "I couldn't do it. I couldn't take him being alive and free while Angelo is . . . dust and ashes. I couldn't . . ."

"It's all right," Clare said. "It's over now. It's all right."

She turned to the three men facing her.

"Nothing happened here," she said. "It was just a misunderstanding."

No one spoke.

"Please." She looked at Neil this time. "Take me and my mother home. Then I have some information for you. I don't know if you can prove it, but I think I've found out who really ran over my brother."

In the corner of the office, Boland was pouring himself a drink. Clare held onto Maria. It was hard to tell which of them was holding the other up. The two police officers looked at each other.

"You're right," Neil said to Clare. "Nothing happened here. Or, if it did, it was over before we arrived. But something happened to you. What?"

"I'll tell you all about it," Clare sighed, as the pain rushed back into her body. "Later."

The four of them left the small office, Clare stumbling as she tried to keep up. Her mother held onto her arm, helping her to walk down the narrow stairs.

23

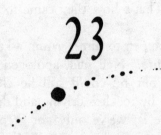

Clare was laid out on the settee. Her legs were exposed, padding and plaster covering the cuts and bruises she had sustained that morning. Her legs were far too fat, she'd always thought. It annoyed her that Neil was seeing her like this, without make-up and nice clothes. But he didn't seem to mind.

"The boy's name is Stephen Baker," Neil told her. "He's in the year above Angelo at Greencoat. He denied everything at first, but we eventually got him to admit to being in the car. He used to be in the Crowston gang. I guess that's where he learnt to take cars. I suspect Crowston knew it was him all along. He was laughing at us.

"Anyway, Stephen claims he wasn't driving, but

won't say who else was with him. Evidently, he – or they – saw Angelo turning onto Bobbers Mill Road and decided to give him a bit of a scare. But there was a mother and child crossing the road, too, and they had to swerve at the last minute to avoid them. That's how they came to knock over Angelo."

"What'll happen to him?" Mum asked.

"I'm not sure," Neil said, apologetically. "He's only fifteen, but he could still be charged with causing death by reckless driving and do up to five years. Trouble is, we've only got Stephen's word for it that he was in the car at all. Angelo's death-bed identification isn't much use, I'm afraid. Evidently the car was burnt out the same day – it was a new blue GTI according to Stephen – so we're unlikely to get any evidence there, even if we're able to trace it. We'll get him, all right, but on a lesser charge."

"How will he be punished?" Dad wanted to know.

"A year or two in a youth detention centre, plus a driving ban from when he's old enough to drive."

"He should be banned for life," Mum said, angrily.

"Maybe," Neil told her, "but magistrates don't like to do that. If the offender knows that he'll never have a licence it gives him no incentive to keep within the law."

"I remember Stephen," Mum said, bitter tears falling down her face. "We gave him a meal once. Angelo was proud to have a friend who was older than him."

"He's just a stupid, frightened kid," Neil told her. "He says he hasn't been near a car since, that he's broken off with his old cronies. For what it's worth, I believe him."

"At least it's resolved," Dad said, quietly. "Now we can begin to pick up the pieces."

"There is one other thing," Neil said to Clare. "The car that knocked you over this morning. I want you to make a statement about it."

"What for?" Clare said.

"We might be able to catch him."

Clare shook her head.

"I don't know the registration number or the make of the car. I don't even think I'd recognize the driver again. I was in shock at the time, remember? So even if you managed to find him, all you'd have to go on would be the scratch on his car."

"That might be enough," Neil said. "And we might find another witness."

"I doubt it," Clare said. "Most probably, what it would come down to is my word against his. Forget it."

"That's not like you," Neil told her.

Clare smiled ruefully.

"Sometimes you need to recognize when you're fighting a lost cause. Then you can save your energy for a fight you have a chance of winning."

"Maybe you're right," Neil told her, getting up to go. "But I had you down as someone who didn't think there was such a thing as a lost cause."

Clare nodded her head abstractedly. Was it right to ignore some injustices and concentrate on others? She didn't know. But she was going to be a policewoman. She was going to find out.

4

Spring

Epilogue

Clare looked in the mirror. Neil was right – the uniform didn't suit her. It flattened her figure, making her look big rather than just tall. Then there was her hair. Most of it had been chopped off the previous day, immediately after they'd fitted her uniform at Sherwood Lodge. Now that it was shorter and thinner, it was less curly, more . . . ordinary. The way it finished, in a short, straight bob around her neck, made Clare's face seem bigger, too. She looked like a different person.

She had become a different person from the one she'd been nine months before. Clare realized that. Her brother was dead and things would never be the same again. She wondered what Angelo would feel if he knew what she was doing now. Pride?

Or embarrassment, at a sister who had taken her quest for justice so seriously?

Someone called her name and Clare remembered where she was. She brushed a hair from her shoulder and walked down into the hall of Epperstone Training College. There was no swearing-in for this job, no graduation ceremony, nothing grand: only a stern-faced sergeant waiting to inspect the appearance of the new intake.

There were fifteen of them: twelve men and three women. Awkwardly, they formed a line, wanting to look each other over, knowing that they shouldn't. They had a week of what was called "familiarization" before they moved on to the regional training college at Ryton, where the real work began.

Clare stood upright, with her hands behind her back, wondering if she looked like a policewoman, wondering what she'd let herself in for. One of the others coughed. Clare began to worry about all this standing still. What if one of her feet went to sleep? Was she allowed to stamp on it? Things started going through her head, things that Neil had told her. Sixty per cent of the job is admin, he insisted. Most of the rest is just standing, or, if you're lucky, sitting around. You can tell the ones who come into the job for idealistic reasons, he warned her. They're the cynical ones with the huge chips on their shoulders.

She'd teased Neil about this when they went out for a drink last night, reminding him of what he'd said to her about lost causes the last time they met, two months before.

"You're the idealistic one," she told him, "not me."

"In that case," he answered, "why are you joining the police force?"

Had Clare given him an answer? No, she had kissed him instead. It had taken her more than six months to kiss him properly, and afterwards he looked like someone who had just experienced a minor earthquake.

"Does this mean you might. . . ?"

Then Clare kissed him again and he got the message. She liked him a lot, though it had taken her a while to realize this, given the tragic circumstances under which they'd met. It was too early for either of them to guess how long they would last. What worried Clare most at this moment was the possibility that she'd confused her interest in Neil with her interest in the job he did.

Why was it that she wanted to do this, of all jobs, more than anything else? Police work, Neil told her last night, had little to do with detection, and even less to do with justice. When he said it, Clare hadn't believed him. However, at this moment, she wasn't so sure. A new chapter in her life was beginning and her head filled with questions, none of which she knew the answer to.

Was Clare ready to change her life so drastically? Would she have been better off finishing her degree first? Would Neil stay keen on her, now that she was keen on him, too? Was it a good idea to have the same job as your boyfriend? Was she good enough?

The inspection began.